Immigration to North America

Indian Immigrants

Tom Balog

Asylum Seekers
Central American Immigrants
Chinese Immigrants
Cuban Immigrants
Indian Immigrants
Mexican Immigrants
Middle Eastern Immigrants
Refugees
Rights & Responsibilities of Citizenship
South American Immigrants
Undocumented Immigration and Homeland Security

Immigration to North America

Indian Immigrants

Tom Balog

Senior Consulting Editor Stuart Anderson
former Associate Commissioner for Policy and Planning,
US. Citizenship and Immigration Services

Introduction by Marian L. Smith, Historian,
U.S. Citizenship and Immigration Services

Introduction by Peter A. Hammerschmidt,
former First Secretary, Permanent Mission of Canada to the United Nations

MASON CREST
PHILADELPHIA

Mason Crest
450 Parkway Drive, Suite D
Broomall, PA 19008
www.masoncrest.com

©2017 by Mason Crest, an imprint of National Highlights, Inc.

All rights reserved. No part of this publication may be reproduced or transmitted in any form or by any means, electronic or mechanical, including photocopying, recording, taping, or any information storage and retrieval system, without permission from the publisher.

Printed and bound in the United States of America.

CPSIA Compliance Information: Batch #INA2016.
For further information, contact Mason Crest at 1-866-MCP-Book.

First printing
1 3 5 7 9 8 6 4 2

Library of Congress Cataloging-in-Publication Data

   on file at the Library of Congress
   ISBN: 978-1-4222-3687-1 (hc)
   ISBN: 978-1-4222-8104-8 (ebook)

Immigration to North America series ISBN: 978-1-4222-3679-6

Table of Contents

Introduction: The Changing Face of the United States	6
by Marian L. Smith	
Introduction: The Changing Face of Canada	10
by Peter A. Hammerschmidt	
1. Indians in North America	15
2. Independence and Conflict	25
3. Immigration to North America	41
4. Making a New Life	59
5. Keeping the Culture Alive	73
6. Human Smuggling and Worker Exploitation	89
7. Future Immigration	95
Famous Indian Americans	100
Series Glossary of Key Terms	102
Further Reading	103
Internet Resources	104
Index	107
Contributors	111

KEY ICONS TO LOOK FOR:

Words to Understand: These words with their easy-to-understand definitions will increase the reader's understanding of the text, while building vocabulary skills.

Sidebars: This boxed material within the main text allows readers to build knowledge, gain insights, explore possibilities, and broaden their perspectives by weaving together additional information to provide realistic and holistic perspectives.

Research Projects: Readers are pointed toward areas of further inquiry connected to each chapter. Suggestions are provided for projects that encourage deeper research and analysis.

Text-Dependent Questions: These questions send the reader back to the text for more careful attention to the evidence presented there.

Series Glossary of Key Terms: This back-of-the book glossary contains terminology used throughout this series. Words found here increase the reader's ability to read and comprehend higher-level books and articles in this field.

The Changing Face of the United States

Marian L. Smith, Historian
U.S. Citizenship and Immigration Services

Americans commonly assume that immigration today is very different than immigration of the past. The immigrants themselves appear to be unlike immigrants of earlier eras. Their language, their dress, their food, and their ways seem strange. At times people fear too many of these new immigrants will destroy the America they know. But has anything really changed? Do new immigrants have any different effect on America than old immigrants a century ago? Is the American fear of too much immigration a new development? Do immigrants really change America more than America changes the immigrants? The very subject of immigration raises many questions.

In the United States, immigration is more than a chapter in a history book. It is a continuous thread that links the present moment to the first settlers on North American shores. From the first colonists' arrival until today, immigrants have been met by Americans who both welcomed and feared them. Immigrant contributions were always welcome—on the farm, in the fields, and in the factories. Welcoming the poor, the persecuted, and the "huddled masses" became an American principle. Beginning with the original Pilgrims' flight from religious persecution in the 1600s, through the Irish migration to escape starvation in the 1800s, to the relocation of Central Americans seeking refuge from civil wars in the 1980s and 1990s, the United States has considered itself a haven for the destitute and the oppressed.

But there was also concern that immigrants would not adopt American ways, habits, or language. Too many immigrants might overwhelm America. If so, the dream of the Founding Fathers for United States government and society would be destroyed. For this reason, throughout American history some have argued that limiting or ending immigration is our patriotic duty. Benjamin Franklin feared there were so many German immigrants in Pennsylvania the Colonial Legislature would begin speaking German. "Progressive" leaders of the early 1900s feared that immigrants who could not read and understand the English language were not only exploited by "big business," but also served as the foundation for "machine politics" that undermined the U.S. Constitution. This theme continues today, usually voiced by those who bear no malice toward immigrants but who want to preserve American ideals.

Have immigrants changed? In colonial days, when most colonists were of English descent, they considered Germans, Swiss, and French immigrants as different. They were not "one of us" because they spoke a different language. Generations later, Americans of German or French descent viewed Polish, Italian, and Russian immigrants as strange. They were not "like us" because they had a different religion, or because they did not come from a tradition of constitutional government. Recently, Americans of Polish or Italian descent have seen Nicaraguan, Pakistani, or Vietnamese immigrants as too different to be included. It has long been said of American immigration that the latest ones to arrive usually want to close the door behind them.

It is important to remember that fear of individual immigrant groups seldom lasted, and always lessened. Benjamin Franklin's anxiety over German immigrants disappeared after those immigrants' sons and daughters helped the nation gain independence in the Revolutionary War. The Irish of the mid-1800s were among the most hated immigrants, but today we all wear green on St. Patrick's Day. While a century ago it was feared that Italian and other Catholic immigrants would vote as directed by the Pope, today that controversy is only a vague memory. Unfortunately, some ethnic groups continue their efforts to earn acceptance. The African

Americans' struggle continues, and some Asian Americans, whose families have been in America for generations, are the victims of current anti-immigrant sentiment.

Time changes both immigrants and America. Each wave of new immigrants, with their strange language and habits, eventually grows old and passes away. Their American-born children speak English. The immigrants' grandchildren are completely American. The strange foods of their ancestors—spaghetti, baklava, hummus, or tofu—become common in any American restaurant or grocery store. Much of what the immigrants brought to these shores is lost, principally their language. And what is gained becomes as American as St. Patrick's Day, Hanukkah, or Cinco de Mayo, and we forget that it was once something foreign.

Recent immigrants are all around us. They come from every corner of the earth to join in the American Dream. They will continue to help make the American Dream a reality, just as all the immigrants who came before them have done.

The Changing Face of Canada

Peter A. Hammerschmidt
former First Secretary, Permanent Mission of Canada to the United Nations

Throughout Canada's history, immigration has shaped and defined the very character of Canadian society. The migration of peoples from every part of the world into Canada has profoundly changed the way we look, speak, eat, and live. Through close and distant relatives who left their lands in search of a better life, all Canadians have links to immigrant pasts. We are a nation built by and of immigrants.

Two parallel forces have shaped the history of Canadian immigration. The enormous diversity of Canada's immigrant population is the most obvious. In the beginning came the enterprising settlers of the "New World," the French and English colonists. Soon after came the Scottish, Irish, and Northern and Central European farmers of the 1700s and 1800s. As the country expanded westward during the mid-1800s, migrant workers began arriving from China, Japan, and other Asian countries. And the turbulent twentieth century brought an even greater variety of immigrants to Canada, from the Caribbean, Africa, India, and Southeast Asia.

So while English- and French-Canadians are the largest ethnic groups in the country today, neither group alone represents a majority of the population. A large and vibrant multicultural mix makes up the rest, particularly in Canada's major cities. Toronto, Vancouver, and Montreal alone are home to people from over 200 ethnic groups!

Less obvious but equally important in the evolution of Canadian immigration has been hope. The promise of a better life lured Europeans and

Americans seeking cheap (sometimes even free) farmland. Thousands of Scots and Irish arrived to escape grinding poverty and starvation. Others came for freedom, to escape religious and political persecution. Canada has long been a haven to the world's dispossessed and disenfranchised—Dutch and German farmers cast out for their religious beliefs, black slaves fleeing the United States, and political refugees of despotic regimes in Europe, Africa, Asia, and South America.

The two forces of diversity and hope, so central to Canada's past, also shaped the modern era of Canadian immigration. Following the Second World War, Canada drew heavily on these influences to forge trailblazing immigration initiatives.

The catalyst for change was the adoption of the Canadian Bill of Rights in 1960. Recognizing its growing diversity and Canadians' changing attitudes towards racism, the government passed a federal statute barring discrimination on the grounds of race, national origin, color, religion, or sex. Effectively rejecting the discriminatory elements in Canadian immigration policy, the Bill of Rights forced the introduction of a new policy in 1962. The focus of immigration abruptly switched from national origin to the individual's potential contribution to Canadian society. The door to Canada was now open to every corner of the world.

Welcoming those seeking new hopes in a new land has also been a feature of Canadian immigration in the modern era. The focus on economic immigration has increased along with Canada's steadily growing economy, but political immigration has also been encouraged. Since 1945, Canada has admitted tens of thousands of displaced persons, including Jewish Holocaust survivors, victims of Soviet crackdowns in Hungary and Czechoslovakia, and refugees from political upheaval in Uganda, Chile, and Vietnam.

Prior to 1978, however, these political refugees were admitted as an exception to normal immigration procedures. That year, Canada revamped its refugee policy with a new Immigration Act that explicitly affirmed Canada's commitment to the resettlement of refugees from oppression. Today, the admission of refugees remains a central part of

Canadian immigration law and regulations.

Amendments to economic and political immigration policy have continued, refining further the bold steps taken during the modern era. Together, these initiatives have turned Canada into one of the world's few truly multicultural states.

Unlike the process of assimilation into a "melting pot" of cultures, immigrants to Canada are more likely to retain their cultural identity, beliefs, and practices. This is the source of some of Canada's greatest strengths as a society. And as a truly multicultural nation, diversity is not seen as a threat to Canadian identity. Quite the contrary—diversity is Canadian identity.

1 Indians in North America

Indian immigrants enrich North American society with their culture, economic and intellectual productivity, strong family values, and work ethics. Most believe they will get ahead by working hard and persevering at whatever they do. Some have succeeded to the point of becoming millionaires, and even billionaires, using equal shares of self-discipline and daring.

Indians and Indian Americans (first- and second-generation immigrants and those descended from immigrants who came a long time ago) make up approximately 1 percent of the U.S. population, according to data from the U.S. Census Bureau. The U.S. Indian population as of 2013, according to Census Bureau data, was about 3.1 million Americans. This total represents an increase of 82 percent over the 1.7 million people of Indian descent reported to be living in the United States in the 2000 census.

In Canada, people of Indian descent are officially labeled in government statistics as Asian Indians, to avoid confusion with the Native American people of Canada. They make up about 4 percent of the national population—approximately 36 million in 2016—meaning that roughly 1.4 million Asian Indians live in Canada.

◀ A growing number of Indians are leaving their homes in South Asia to resettle in North America. Indian Americans fall behind the Filipinos and the Chinese in population size, but they comprise the fastest-growing Asian American group. In Canada, Indians are the largest immigrant group behind the Chinese.

These immigrants arriving to North America have traveled thousands of miles from their homeland, the Republic of India, which occupies a little less than 1.3 million square miles (3,287,590 square kilometers) of southern Asia. India is bordered on the west by the Arabian Sea and Pakistan; on the north by China, Nepal, and Bhutan; and on the east by the Bay of Bengal, Bangladesh, and Myanmar (formerly known as Burma). Just over one-third the size of the United States, India is home to over 1.25 billion people, making it the second most populous nation in the world. More than three-quarters of the Indian population practices the Hindu faith.

Indians generally come to North America in search of better professional opportunities and a better life for their children, though a small segment of the population comes hoping to escape persecution or dangerous conditions in their homeland. Although the number of Indians in North America is only a small percentage of the overall population, the Indian population is growing rapidly. In fact, its average annual growth rate of 7.6 percent is the largest of all the Asian American groups. Indians make up 16.4 percent of the Asian American community in North America, and have recently passed Filipinos to become the second-largest Asian-American group, behind only the Chinese.

Each year the United States welcomes roughly 65,000 to 70,000 immigrants from India, according to the *Yearbook of Immigration Statistics*. In the most recent years for which complete data is available, 63,320 Indians were admitted to the United States in 2012 and 65,506 in 2013. The only countries

 Words to Understand in This Chapter

ashram—a spiritual center, often used for yoga or other Hindu disciplines.
mehndi—ancient henna tattoo body art.
swami—a Hindu religious teacher.

Many Indian immigrants come to the United States and Canada to work in the computer industry as programmers and managers.

that provided a greater number of immigrants to the United States in those years were Mexico and China.

In 2014, Canada opened its doors to 38,341 Indians, making them the second-largest immigrant group that year, behind Filipinos. Typically Canada admits 30,000 to 40,000 Asian Indians per year to become lawful permanent residents.

Highly Successful Immigrants

Most Indian immigrants are middle or upper class, well educated, and English-speaking. According to a report by the Embassy of India in Washington, D.C., more than 87 percent of Indian immigrants in the U.S. have a high school diploma, and some 62 to 75 percent hold at least a bachelor's degree (compared with the 21 percent of the overall U.S. population who hold a bachelor's degree). Even many of those Indians lacking the formal education of the immigrant group's majority have had success buy-

Hinduism in North America

In 1893, 30-year-old Hindu Swami Vivekananda (1863–1902) introduced North Americans to the Hindu religion and yoga. Arriving as a missionary dressed in turban and robes, he addressed the World Parliament of Religions at the 1893 Chicago Columbia Exposition. All world religions were supposed to be represented at the fair, yet no Hindu had been invited, and the swami was nearly prohibited from speaking. But once he stepped on stage and addressed the audience, he received a standing ovation. Vivekananda discussed religious tolerance and unity, a theme he continued to expound upon over the next seven years of his lecturing in the United States and Britain.

The swami preached the Vedanta philosophy, a Hindu set of fundamental principles maintaining that all religious traditions are equal and man's true nature is divine. Vivekananda founded the Vedanta Society, which operates 20 ashrams, or spiritual centers, in the United States, as well as one in Canada. Traditionally, membership has been white, but more Indians have joined following the increase in immigration during the 1990s.

Hindu immigrants make up half of New York City's Vedanta Society membership. The society runs summer camps where Hindu children socialize with kids of similar backgrounds. They are exposed to religious beliefs, values, and traditions and learn how to chant prayers, feel comfortable in a temple, and practice yoga. Hinduism has become the world's third-largest religion, behind Christianity and Islam. Worldwide, more than one billion people practice Hinduism. More than 2.2 million of these Hindus live in the United States, making it the country's fourth-largest faith, and about 500,000 more live in Canada as of 2016.

This ornate Hindu temple is located in Atlanta, Georgia.

ing or starting up thriving businesses.

The economic status that Indian Americans have reached is a good indicator of their success. Their annual buying power is estimated at $40 billion, and their per capita income is more than twice that of the general population. The Embassy of India reported that the median family income of Indians in the U.S. was $60,093 in 2000, compared to the national family median income of $38,885. Almost half of all Indian Americans work in management or professional occupations, with about one-third working in technical, sales, and administrative positions. About 300,000 work in the San Jose–Palo Alto area of California, better known as "Silicon Valley," where technology jobs offer a median income of around $150,000 a year. More than 5,000 Indian Americans are faculty members of colleges and universities. According to a report in Time Select/Global Business Report magazine, only 6 percent of Indian immigrants live in poverty. Fewer than 1 percent receive public assistance.

Indian American girls try *falooda kulfi*, an Indian dish similar to ice cream. Traditional Indian foods can be found in most cities in the United States and Canada.

One Indian traditional fashion that has found particular favor among Americans and Canadians is *mehndi*, an elaborate style of semi-permanent markings applied on the hands and other parts of the body. *Mehndi* particularly became a fashionable trend among non-Indians during the 1990s. In traditional Indian households, *mehndi* designs are placed on a bride in preparation for marriage.

Indian Influence on Western Culture

The presence of Indians in North America has exposed Westerners to a variety of cultural traditions, ranging from food and fashion to philosophies on religion and health.

Today, most North American cities and towns have Indian restaurants. They offer a variety of traditional foods, many of them vegetarian (prepared without meat). One popular dish, *navratan korma*, consists of five vegetables in a cream sauce, cooked by the *Balti* method. The word *Balti* refers to the large pot in which the food is cooked over high heat. Other popular Indian foods include *tandoori* chicken, chicken curry, and *nan*, Indian flat bread.

Trendy coffeehouses such as Starbucks serve the Indian drink *chai*, a strong and heavily spiced tea. According to legend, *chai* was created for a king in India who thought it was such a luxury that he would not allow it to be served outside his court. The blend of black teas is seasoned with cinnamon, cardamom, cloves, ginger, nutmeg, honey, and milk. Coffeehouses serve it iced or hot with a cinnamon stick or whipped cream. Health food stores sell *chai* in liquid concentrate, powder mix, or loose tea form.

Many Westerners have adopted Indian fashion, in a number of cases for the sake of fun and style and not for its religious or cultural significance. For example, beginning in the 1990s an "Indo-chic" trend became popular. T-shirts portrayed images of Hindu gods. Westerners sported **mehndi**, elaborate tattoos made from a special paste called henna—in Indian tradition *mehndi* designs are placed on a bride in preparation for marriage. American beauty salons applied elaborate semi-permanent designs. Celebrities popularized the wearing of the *bindi*, a distinctive round red dot worn by Indian brides. In keeping with the *bindis* style, Westerners also placed self-stick gemstones on their foreheads. In the late 1990s, these gemstones moved to other parts of the body with stenciled designs painted around them.

Bringing India to America

Children's writer Dhan Gopal Mukerji (1890–1936) arrived in the United States penniless in 1910. To pay his tuition at the University of California, he took menial jobs and unskilled farm and factory work.

Mukerji worked his way to become the first South Asian immigrant with a successful literary career, writing books that wove together Indian lore, culture, and religion. In 1928, he became the first Asian and only Indian to win the American Library Association's prestigious Newbery Medal for children's literature. He received the award for his 1927 book *Gay Neck: the Story of a Pigeon*, which was based on his childhood experiences in Calcutta. Mukerji wrote nine children's books of animal stories, including *Kari the Elephant*, in 1922, and *Ghond the Hunter*, in 1928.

The author's total output includes more than 20 books spanning fiction, nonfiction, poetry, drama, and translations. Mukerji's 1923 biography, *Caste and Outcast*, introduced many Americans to India's landscape and culture. The book contrasts Hindu spirituality and life in India with the materialism of the West. It has been reprinted and translated many times.

A public yoga event in New York City's Times Square. This form of exercise that developed in India has become very popular in the United States and other Western countries.

With the growth of the Indian immigrant population has also come much exposure of Hindu beliefs and philosophies to Westerners. In the 1970s Maharishi Mahesh Yogi, a guru to the famous rock group the Beatles, introduced ayurveda to the United States. Ayurveda, the Hindu science of life, comes from the Sanskrit words for "life" and "knowledge." (Sanskrit is the ancient sacred and literary language of India.) The word *ayurveda* literally means "wisdom of life," and has been a major philosophy and medical system throughout Indian history, handed down orally and through Sanskrit poetry.

To ensure one's health, well-being, and longevity, ayurveda emphasizes harmony between mind, body, and spirit. The basic beliefs of ayurveda establish three underlying *doshas*, or mind-body principles—*kapha*, *vata*, and *pitta*. From birth, the *doshas* are in force, influencing human traits ranging from skin type to personality. Balancing all three *doshas* through meditation, nutrition, exercise, herbal formulas, surgery, and yoga ensures health and beauty.

Ayurveda has become a commercial success in America, with the opening of ayurvedic spas and the marketing of a variety of ayurvedic products made from Indian oils and herbs. Ayurvedic herbal compounds are used in the manufacture of some lip protectors and sunscreens.

Yoga is based on the ancient principle that the body is the temple of the spirit. A popular form of exercise, yoga attributes good health to spiritual growth through stress reduction. Growing numbers of yoga classes are taught today in neighborhood YMCAs and community centers.

Text-Dependent Questions

1. What is the percentage of Indian Americans in the U.S. population? What is the percentage in the Canadian population?
2. In what part of California do many Indian immigrants work?

Research Project

Using a library or the Internet, research one of India's provinces or autonomous regions. In a box, present the following basic information: Total area; Highest point; Lowest point; Population; Capital city; Other major cities. Then write a three- or four- paragraph essay on unique aspects or special issues facing the province or autonomous region.

2 Independence and Conflict

India is a complex country of contrasts. It is home to the very rich and the very poor, the well educated and the illiterate. Its cities boast advanced technology while its villages lack basic utilities. Birthplace of leader Mohandas Gandhi, who advocated change through nonviolent resistance, the country has seen a great deal of progress since achieving independence in 1947. However, India has also had great difficulty in keeping pace economically, and in recent decades has experienced riots and acts of terrorism.

The history of India dates back many centuries. Known as Bharat in ancient times, the Indus River Valley was invaded by Aryan tribes around 1500 BCE. The resulting merger of the Aryan and native civilizations gave birth to classical Indian culture and the Hindu religion. (Today, about 72 percent of India's population is Indo-Aryan, according to the U.S. State Department.) In the 10th and 11th centuries, invading Turks and Afghans brought the Islamic faith to India, which became popular among many Indians.

Around 1619, the British-owned East India Company began setting up trading stations throughout the country. By the 1850s, Great Britain controlled most of present-day India, Pakistan, and Bangladesh. Modern India's culture, educational

◀ Pedestrians pass slowly through a crowded street of Old Delhi. India is the second-most populous country in the world today, with more than 1.25 billion people. It faces many problems, including overcrowding, environmental pollution, and widespread poverty.

institutions, and government reflect the years of British influence. In the early 1920s, Gandhi, an outspoken spiritual leader, led a movement against the British that eventually led to India winning its independence in August 1947.

India's constitution, adopted in January 1950, established a federal government modeled on Great Britain's parliamentary system. India's democracy is similar to the U.S. system but gives the central government more power over individual states.

Language and People

India is the second-most populous country in the world, with over 1.25 billion people in 2016. This represents 17.5 percent (or more than one-sixth) of the world population. At an annual growth rate of 1.2 percent, the United Nations projects that by 2022, India will surpass China to become the world's most populous nation.

Hindi is the most widely used language of India, spoken by over 422 million people. About 10 percent of the population—roughly 125 million people—speak fluent English in addition to an Indian language. Most English-speakers are well-educated, as it is the language used for international business and politics. India recognizes 14 other official languages, although more than 1,500 languages and dialects are spoken.

Some 30 percent of the population lives in 200 cities and towns. These include the capital, New Delhi, with a population of 11 million; Mumbai (formerly called Bombay), a western sea-

 Words to Understand in This Chapter

caste—social position or class assigned at birth in the Hindu religion.

refugee—an alien outside the United States who is unable or unwilling to return to his or her country of nationality because of persecution or a well-founded fear of persecution.

gross domestic product (GDP)—an economic term that measures the total value of domestic goods and services produced by a country within the course of a year.

26 **Indian Immigrants**

Students attend their local school in Raxaul, Bihar. The state of Bihar is one of the poorest in India.

port and India's largest city, with a population of 15 million; and the eastern port of Calcutta, with a population of 5 million. The other 70 percent of the population consists mostly of farmers, who live in over 550,000 rural villages scattered through the country. India's modern cities of high-rise buildings and quality schools stand in stark contrast to its poorer villages, which may lack electricity, running water, and telephone service.

A Land of Many Faiths

Hindus and Muslims constitute the largest religious groups in India. About 1 billion people, about 80 percent of the country's population, are Hindu. Twelve to 15 percent are Muslims. Estimated to number from 150 to 190 million, they make up the world's second-largest Muslim community outside Indonesia. About 2.3 percent of Indians are Christians, with roughly two-thirds of them adhering to the Roman Catholic faith. The rest of

Spiritual and political leader Mohandas Gandhi (1869–1948) helped India gain independence after nearly three and a half centuries of British colonial rule. Gandhi also was a vocal critic of India's oppressive caste system.

the country's population observes Sikh, Jain, Buddhist, or Parsi religious beliefs.

In India, religion, language, and—for Hindus—*caste* are determining factors of an individual's social position, education, career, and future. The Hindu caste system encompasses four categories: priest or scholar, warrior, merchant, and laborer. Within these categories are thousands of castes and subcastes. Being born into a certain caste can limit someone's opportunities since the system dictates that jobs and social status be assigned at birth. Entire villages may be segregated by caste.

Outcasts, or "untouchables," rank at the bottom of the system. Gandhi, an opponent of the caste system, called members of this caste "Harijan" (children of God). Today they prefer to be known today as *Dalits*, the Hindi word meaning "the oppressed." About 16 percent of India's population, or an estimated 160 million people, are Dalits. They have no access to education and are forbidden to drink at wells of the upper caste or worship at their temples. Their life's work usually involves tasks considered religiously impure by the higher classes, such as cleaning toilets or handling animal carcasses. While some Dalits have escaped the social system, advancement is extremely difficult, especially in villages. Dalits may blend into the anonymity of larger cities or convert to other religions.

In 1950 the government outlawed the caste system, and provided agricultural subsidies and scholarships to untouchables. Although laws prohibit discrimination and slots are reserved for Dalits in parliament, state legislatures, government offices, and schools, the laws are not always followed and the caste system remains resistant to change.

Conflicts Between Social and Religious Factions

Muslims and Hindus have proven capable of living peacefully as neighbors, but the goal of multicultural tolerance has not always been achieved. Recent years have seen the rise of many religious, militant, and separatist organizations and an escalation of violence. While most Indians and India's government condemn the violence, riotous outbreaks and retaliatory attacks continue.

Hindu nationalism, a movement based on the belief that Hindus come first and all other groups are secondary, has been rising since the late 1980s. The Hindu nationalist Bharatiya Janata Party, led by Prime Minister Atal Bihari Vajpayee, came into power in March 1998. In a move upheld by India's supreme court, Hindu nationalists are rewriting school history texts from their perspective. New editions of books delete references to such historical truths as the 1948 assassination of Gandhi by a Hindu extremist, the oppressive effects of the caste system, and the Hindus' criticisms of certain ethnic groups and religious leaders.

For over a century the small town of Ayodhya, located in the state of Uttar Pradesh, has been the scene of violent altercations between Muslims and Hindus. The beginning of the friction dates back to 1528, the year when Muslim Emperor Mir Baqi dismantled an 11th-century Hindu temple marking what some believed to be the birthplace of the Hindu god Rama. The emperor had the Babri Mosque constructed over the site. Hindus and Muslims continued to dispute the site's rightful ownership. Rioting broke out in 1855, and 75 people died in the violence.

Subsequent riots in 1934 damaged the mosque, which was later repaired. After Hindus raided and took over the mosque in December 1949, the government locked up the building and declared it off limits. The following year, Hindus and Muslims both petitioned the courts for possession. After over three decades the mosque reopened in 1986; during the same time groundbreaking ceremonies were held for a Hindu temple to be built adjacent to the mosque. Riots broke out shortly afterward, during which 600 people died. Hundreds were killed in another outburst that occurred in 1990.

In December 1992 the conflict was re-ignited, as a mob of 4,000 Hindus, using their bare hands, pickaxes, metal rods, and sledgehammers, destroyed the 464-year-old mosque in just nine hours. After police finally drove away the attackers with stakes and tear gas, the mob then decided to destroy other Muslim structures, looting and burning about 270 Muslim homes and destroying 18 other local mosques. Eventually, rioting spread to at least 1,000 villages throughout India, Pakistan, and Bangladesh. More than 1,100 were dead and 4,000 injured. Hindu temples were destroyed. Hundreds more perished in subsequent rioting that erupted in Mumbai.

Hindu-Muslim hostilities continued to simmer, erupting again 10 years later. In February 2002, the Sabarmati Express, a train carrying Hindu pilgrims returning from Ayodhya stopped just after dawn at Godhra, in western India. A waiting Muslim mob surrounded the train, poured gas into a car carrying mostly women passengers, and set fire to it. In the attack 58 people were burned alive. Days later, a Hindu mob retaliated by torching a Muslim housing complex in the town of Gujarat.

A Muslim kneels in prayer in the town of Srinagar, India. Muslims comprise 12 to 15 percent of the total Indian population. Indians also follow the Hindu, Sikh, Jain, Buddhist, Parsi, and Christian faiths.

The violence continued for weeks. Hundreds of Muslims and dozens of Hindus were killed, and hundreds of thousands of Muslims were displaced. Countless numbers of mosques and other religious and culturally important places have been damaged or destroyed in violent outbreaks that still occur today.

Along with the persistent friction between Hindus and Muslims, Hindus and Christians have also clashed in recent years. In the late 1990s, Christians became targets of brutal attacks. Hindu extremists accused missionaries of converting poor low-caste Hindus by enticing them with Western money. Some regarded this as a Christian conspiracy to take over India; others believed upper-caste Hindu militants feared losing their economic advantages over the lower classes. Anti-Christian violence has included attacks on priests and nuns, church bombings, and the vandalizing of Christian graveyards. A network of Hindu groups known as the Sangh Parivar (United Family) is believed responsible for much of the hostility. Some of its leaders want Christians expelled from India, although most deny any wrongdoing.

Violence has also erupted in India between Hindus and the Sikh population. Sikhs represent a small, relatively prosperous minority, about 2 percent of the Indian population. Militant separatist groups want the state of Punjab, where Sikhs form a slight majority, turned into an independent Sikh state called Khalistan. These extremists have tried to force their 14 million Hindu neighbors to leave the region. In June 1984, government army troops stormed the Sikhs' holiest shrine, the Golden Temple at Amritsar, after armed Sikh radicals barricaded themselves inside. An estimated 1,000 people died, the majority of whom were Sikhs.

After two Sikh bodyguards assassinated Prime Minister Indira Gandhi on October 31, 1984, anti-Sikh riots erupted in New Delhi. Hindu mobs burned Sikhs alive, and an estimated 2,000 Sikhs were massacred during the violence. In May 1985, India suffered its worst terrorist attack since achieving independence. At least 19 explosions devastated public places throughout New Delhi and nearby states, killing 79 people, many of them children, and injuring over 100 people. Police blamed Sikh terrorists for planting bombs in transistor radios that exploded when passersby picked them up and turned them on. Bloodshed continued in the state of Punjab through 1995. In September of that year, after a car bomb killed the state's chief minister, Beant Singh, the police and the army cracked down on Sikh radicals.

Conflict with Pakistan

For more than 60 years, India has been at odds with neighboring Pakistan, where most of the population is Muslim. Immediately after the partition of India and Pakistan, a war broke out between the two countries in which an estimated 250,000 people were killed. A major refugee crisis also developed, during which large numbers of Hindus and Sikhs left

Indian soldiers set out on a routine patrol near the village of Rangdum, in the disputed province of Jammu and Kashmir. In 2014 and 2015 Indian and Pakistani troops were engaged in several skirmishes in Kashmir along the border between the two countries.

Pakistan and moved to India. At the same time, Muslims fled India for Pakistan. Historians estimate that more than 12 million people became refugees immediately after the 1947 partition. Meanwhile, Hindu-Muslim violence continued to break out, especially in Punjab. People were beaten to death with clubs and stones. Over four months, an estimated 500,000 to 1 million people were killed.

Disputes over certain regions—particularly Jammu and Kashmir, a province of India with a Muslim majority that has been claimed by Pakistan—have been violent and continuous, erupting into full-fledged war in 1965 and again in 1971. The world has viewed the tense relationship between the two countries with great anxiety, and the United States and other world powers have involved themselves in peace negotiations.

The situation between India and Pakistan has become more dangerous since 1998, when Pakistan developed nuclear

Pakistanis demonstrate against the Indian presence in Kashmir. The relationship between the two nations has historically been very tense.

weapons. (India first developed nuclear weapons in the 1970s.) A full-scale war between these longtime adversaries now has the potential for millions of deaths and nuclear devastation throughout Central and Southern Asia. Today, security agencies estimate that India possesses about 100 nuclear weapons, while Pakistan's nuclear arsenal is estimated at between 100 and 120 weapons.

Recent years have shown both hopeful signs and increased hostilities between Pakistan and India over Kashmir. A major cease-fire was reached in November 2003 and peace talks occurred in January 2004.

Complicating the peace efforts, however, have been recent attacks in India largely blamed on Pakistani militants. Many targets have been religious sites, including bombings in 2006 at a temple in the ancient pilgrimage city of Varanasi and an attack at a mosque in the southern city of Hyderabad in 2007. In July

2008, a series of explosions ripped through the western city of Ahmedabad in India, killing at least 45 people and wounding 160. Then, in November 2008, ten Pakistani gunmen terrorized Mumbai, attacking hotels, cafés, a railway station, and a hospital. The attacks killed 166 people and injured hundreds more. The confirmation that these men were Pakistani citizens halted all peace negotiations and reinforced a notion that Islamic terrorists are to blame for violence in India.

Finally in 2012, Indian Prime Minister Manmohan Singh and Pakistani President Asif Ali Zardari broke the seven-year silence with high-level talks. However, little was accomplished. Prime Minister Nawaz Sharif has promised a new era of relations between the countries, but India refuses to engage in peace talks while Pakistani militants continue to break the cease-fire. In 2014 and 2015, cross-border firing and occasional skirmishes between Indian and Pakistani troops in Kashmir marked the worst violence in a decade.

Pollution, Natural Catastrophe, and Poverty

Today, Indians face many challenges. The country is subject to natural disasters such as floods, droughts, and powerful storms called cyclones (hurricanes), and these often cause enormous losses of life and damage to property.

For example, in 1999 a heat wave in New Delhi killed hundreds of people, while thousands more died from cases of gastroenteritis and cholera that were brought on from drinking contaminated water). In 2015, massive flooding killed hundreds of people in India.

Apart from these natural threats, India is also faced with long-standing pollution issues and infrastructure crises. Several factors combine to make the residential zones of India's cities unappealing. Mumbai's slums are the largest of Asia, and half of the population does not have access to running water. In Mumbai, as in most of India's largest cities, open cooking fires, auto rickshaws (covered two-wheeled vehicles), taxis, diesel buses, and coal-fired power plants pol-

A cycle rickshaw transports a passenger through a flooded street in Varanasi, India. The country is subject to heavy flooding during the annual monsoon season. Indians also face other weather extremes, such as heat waves and droughts.

lute the air. A large number of Indians ride gasoline- and oil-powered motor scooters, which produce more smog than automobiles. The bad air causes sore throats and allergies.

In some parts of India the water is undrinkable because raw sewage, industrial waste, and the runoff of agricultural pesticides have polluted the rivers. In heavily farmed areas, deforestation and overgrazing have caused soil erosion and desert-like conditions.

Although India's education system produces a segment of well-educated people, many never receive the instruction they need. The government provides free public education, with the requirement that students attend school through age 14, yet hundreds of thousands of children complete less than five years before dropping out. With child labor legal in India, some 100 million children under 14 are working. Almost half the people over the age of 15 are illiterate (unable to read and write). About

56 percent of the men are literate, while only 38 percent of the women can read and write. In some regions, women receive no education, and in the state of Rajasthan only about 5 percent of the women are literate.

In terms of **gross domestic product** (GDP), which measures the value of all final goods and services produced within a nation in a given year, India ranks fourth at $8 trillion in 2015. That year it was behind only China ($19.5 trillion), the European Union ($19.2 trillion), and the United States ($17.9 trillion), and ahead of economic powerhouses like Japan ($4.6 trillion) and Russia ($3.4 trillion). However, the figure is less impressive when viewed on a per-capita basis. By that measure, India ranks 158 out of 230 countries, in the same area as other lower-income countries like Bolivia, Nigeria, and Vietnam. About 30 percent of Indians live in poverty, surviving on less than $2 per day.

Poor men wait on the street for a job in Calcutta. India has the largest number of people living below the poverty line of $1.25 per day.

Independence and Conflict

Small textile factories such as this one in Delhi provide inexpensive clothes to Western countries like the United States and Canada.

Technology Exporter

A sizable number of those Indians who do receive a good education hail from, or set up business in, the city of Bangalore. The capital of the state of Karnataka, Bangalore is known as India's "Silicon State." Home to advanced high-technology firms, it is a city of high-rises and plush modern office complexes. Colleges in Bangalore turn out approximately 30,000 engineering graduates per year. Limited opportunities in India have made the country a major exporter of computer and technical workers. An information technology job pays about $1,000 per month in India, compared to the $75,000 or more per year that many tech companies pay their employees in North America.

Today India also exports services that are delivered by telephone and the Internet. These services include accounting, telemarketing, helpdesk support, medical transcription, payroll management, claims processing, credit evaluation services, engineering design, animation, and maintaining databases. With a skilled and English-speaking labor force that works for lower wages, Indian companies undercut competitors by 30 to 40 percent, according to a Reuters business report. Operators who speak English with an American or neutral accent are trained in American culture and adopt American names so that callers often do not realize they are speaking to someone outside the United States. More than half of America's Fortune 500 companies have contracted Indian technology support. Indian call centers generate about $7 billion in revenue annually.

Text-Dependent Questions

1. In what year did India become independent?
2. What is the most widely spoken language in India?
3. What is the caste system?

Research Project

Using library resources or the Internet, find out more about the partition of India in 1947. If possible, read first-person accounts of Indian and Pakistani people who lived through that turbulent period. List the five most surprising things you learned.

3 Immigration to North America

Often referred to as a "nation of immigrants," the United States has become a popular destination for Indian immigrants. The same is true for Canada—especially in recent years, as Indians have become one of the largest immigrant groups. In both countries, there has been a gradual historic move toward an "open-door" immigration policy regarding Indians. However, there have also been periods when the reception of Indian immigrants has been cooler than in other years. To have a better understanding of what has caused these changes in policy, it is important to briefly examine the history of immigration to North America.

A Short History of U.S. Immigration

Immigration to the United States has been characterized by openness punctuated by periods of restriction. During the 17th, 18th, and 19th centuries, immigration was essentially open without restriction, and, at times, immigrants were even recruited to come to America. Between 1783 and 1820, approximately 250,000 immigrants arrived at U.S. shores. Between 1841 and 1860, more than 4 million immigrants came; most were from England, Ireland, and Germany.

◀ An Asian immigrant mother waits in an airport with her two children. Before the 1960s, restrictive quotas and the great distance between South Asia and North America resulted in low immigration numbers from India. Since the important legislative acts of that decade, however, immigration has been more open, and the Indian American and Indian Canadian population has grown dramatically.

Historically, race and ethnicity have played a role in legislation to restrict immigration. The Chinese Exclusion Act of 1882, which was not repealed until 1943, specifically prevented Chinese people from becoming U.S. citizens and did not allow Chinese laborers to immigrate for the next decade. An agreement with Japan in the early 1900s prevented most Japanese immigration to the United States.

Until the 1920s, no numerical restrictions on immigration existed in the United States, although health restrictions applied. The only other significant restrictions came in 1917, when passing a literacy test became a requirement for immigrants. Presidents Cleveland, Taft, and Wilson had vetoed similar measures earlier. In addition, in 1917 a prohibition was added to the law against the immigration of people from Asia (defined as the Asiatic barred zone). While a few of these prohibitions were lifted during World War II, they were not repealed until 1952, and even then Asians were only allowed in under very small annual quotas.

U.S. Immigration Policy from World War I to 1965

During World War I, the federal government required that all travelers to the United States obtain a *visa* at a U.S. consulate or diplomatic post abroad. As former State Department consular affairs officer C. D. Scully points out, by making that requirement permanent Congress, by 1924, established the framework

 Words to Understand in This Chapter

deportation—forced removal of someone from a country, usually back to his or her native land.
eugenics—the study, now derided as a false science, of attempting to "improve" the human race through breeding; often used as a cover for racial discrimination.
visa—official authorization that permits arrival at a port of entry but does not guarantee admission into the United States.

A STATUE FOR *OUR* HARBOR.

A satirical cartoon entitled "A Statue for *Our* Harbor," printed in an 1881 issue of the San Francisco–based magazine *The Wasp*, represents the anti-immigration perspective of many Americans during the 19th century. The cartoon attributes a number of social problems, including immorality, disease, filth, and the ruin of "white labor," to Chinese immigrants. The drawing appeared a year before Congress passed the Chinese Exclusion Act of 1882, which prohibited the Chinese from immigrating to the United States.

of temporary, or non-immigrant visas (for study, work, or travel), and immigrant visas (for permanent residence). That framework remains in place today.

After World War I, cultural intolerance and bizarre racial theories led to new immigration restrictions. The House Judiciary Committee employed a *eugenics* consultant, Dr. Harry N. Laughlin, who asserted that certain races were inferior. Another leader of the eugenics movement, Madison Grant, argued that Jews, Italians, and others were inferior because of their supposedly different skull size.

The Immigration Act of 1924, preceded by the Temporary Quota Act of 1921, set new numerical limits on immigration based on "national origin." Taking effect in 1929, the 1924 act set annual quotas on immigrants that were specifically designed to keep out southern Europeans, such as Italians and Greeks. Generally no more than 100 people of the proscribed nationalities were permitted to immigrate.

While the new law was rigid, the U.S. Department of State's restrictive interpretation directed consular officers overseas to be even stricter in their application of the "public charge" provision. (A public charge is someone unable to support himself or

Many immigrants from Asia were processed at Angel Island, a facility located in San Francisco Bay. The station there, sometimes called the "Ellis Island of the West," operated from 1910 to 1940.

his family.) As author Laura Fermi wrote, "In response to the new cry for restriction at the beginning of the [Great Depression] . . . the consuls were to interpret very strictly the clause prohibiting admission of aliens 'likely to become public charges; and to deny the visa to an applicant who in their opinion might become a public charge at any time.'"

In the early 1900s, more than one million immigrants a year came to the United States. In 1930—the first year of the national-origin quotas—approximately 241,700 immigrants were admitted. But under the State Department's strict interpretations, only 23,068 immigrants entered during 1933, the smallest total since 1831. Later these restrictions prevented many Jews in Germany and elsewhere in Europe from escaping what would become the Holocaust. At the height of the Holocaust in 1943, the United States admitted fewer than 6,000 refugees.

The Displaced Persons Act of 1948, the nation's first refugee law, allowed many refugees from World War II to settle in the United States. The law put into place policy changes that had already seen immigration rise from 38,119 in 1945 to 108,721 in 1946 (and later to 249,187 in 1950). One-third of those admitted between 1948 and 1951 were Poles, with ethnic Germans forming the second-largest group.

The 1952 Immigration and Nationality Act is best known for its restrictions against those who supported communism or anarchy. However, the bill's other provisions were quite restrictive and were passed over the veto of President Truman. The 1952 act retained the national-origin quota system for the Eastern Hemisphere. The Western Hemisphere continued to operate without a quota and relied on other qualitative factors to limit immigration. Moreover, during that time, the Mexican bracero program, from 1942 to 1964, allowed millions of Mexican agricultural workers to work temporarily in the United States.

The 1952 act set aside half of each national quota to be divided among three preference categories for relatives of U.S. citizens and permanent residents. The other half went to aliens with high education or exceptional abilities. These quotas applied only to those from the Eastern Hemisphere.

A Halt to the National-Origin Quotas

The Immigration and Nationality Act of 1965 became a landmark in immigration legislation by specifically striking the racially based national-origin quotas. It removed the barriers to Asian immigration, which later led to opportunities to immigrate for many Filipinos, Chinese, Koreans, and others. The Western Hemisphere was designated a ceiling of 120,000 immigrants but without a preference system or per country limits. Modifications made in 1978 ultimately combined the Western and Eastern Hemispheres into one preference system and one ceiling of 290,000.

The 1965 act built on the existing system—without the national-origin quotas—and gave somewhat more priority to family relationships. It did not completely overturn the existing system but rather carried forward essentially intact the family immigration categories from the 1959 amendments to the Immigration and Nationality Act. Even though the text of the law prior to 1965 indicated that half of the immigration slots were reserved for skilled employment immigration, in practice, Immigration and Naturalization Service (INS) statistics show that 86 percent of the visas issued between 1952 and 1965 went for family immigration.

A number of significant pieces of legislation since 1980 have shaped the current U.S. immigration system. First, the Refugee Act of 1980 removed refugees from the annual world limit and established that the president would set the number of refugees who could be admitted each year after consultations with Congress.

Second, the 1986 Immigration Reform and Control Act (IRCA) introduced sanctions against employers who "knowing-

The 1965 Immigration and Nationality Act, signed by President Lyndon Johnson, was one of the century's most significant immigration acts. With its employment preferences and priorities granted to family members, the act created resettlement opportunities for thousands of newcomers from India and other Asian countries.

ly" hired undocumented immigrants (those here illegally). It also provided amnesty for many undocumented immigrants.

Third, the Immigration Act of 1990 increased legal immigration by 40 percent. In particular, the act significantly increased the number of employment-based immigrants (to 140,000), while also boosting family immigration.

Fourth, the 1996 Illegal Immigration Reform and Immigrant Responsibility Act (IIRAIRA) significantly tightened rules that permitted undocumented immigrants to convert to legal status and made other changes that tightened immigration law in areas such as political asylum and *deportation.*

Fifth, in response to the September 11, 2001, terrorist attacks, the USA PATRIOT Act and the Enhanced Border Security and Visa Entry Reform Act tightened rules on the granting of visas to individuals from certain countries and enhanced the federal government's monitoring and detention authority over foreign nationals in the United States.

New U.S. Immigration Agencies

In a dramatic reorganization of the federal government, the Homeland Security Act of 2002 abolished the Immigration and Naturalization Service and transferred its immigration service and enforcement functions from the Department of Justice into a new Department of Homeland Security. The Customs Service, the Coast Guard, and parts of other agencies were also transferred into the new department.

The Department of Homeland Security, with regards to immigration, is organized as follows: The bureau of Customs and Border Protection (CBP) contains Customs and Immigration inspectors, who check the documents of travelers to the United States at air, sea, and land ports of entry; and Border Patrol agents, the uniformed agents who seek to prevent unlawful entry along the southern and northern border. The new bureau of Immigration and Customs Enforcement (ICE) employs investigators, who attempt to find undocumented immigrants inside the United States, and Detention and Removal officers, who

President Bush signs the Enhanced Border Security and Visa Entry Reform Act with congressional members in attendance, May 2002. The act, along with the USA PATRIOT Act, was passed in response to the September 2001 terrorist attacks.

detain and seek to deport such individuals. The new bureau of Citizenship and Immigration Services (USCIS) is where people go, or correspond with, to become U.S. citizens or obtain permission to work or extend their stay in the United States.

Following the terrorist attacks of September 11, 2001, the Department of Justice adopted several measures that did not require new legislation to be passed by Congress. Some of these measures created controversy and raised concerns about civil liberties. For example, FBI and INS agents detained for months more than 1,000 foreign nationals of Middle Eastern descent and refused to release the names of the individuals. It is alleged that the Department of Justice adopted tactics that discouraged the detainees from obtaining legal assistance. The Department of Justice also began requiring foreign nationals from primarily Muslim nations to be fingerprinted and questioned by immigration officers upon entry or if they have been living in the United States. Those involved in the September 11 attacks were not immigrants—people who become permanent residents with a right to stay in the United States—but holders of temporary visas, primarily visitor or tourist visas.

Immigration to the United States Today

From the 1920s to the 1960s, the rate of legal immigration to the United States was kept low. Since the immigration law changes of the mid-1960s, the number of foreign-born people in the United States has been rising steadily. The foreign-born population was about 9.6 million according to the 1970 census. This was 4.7 percent of the total U.S. population. That number, as well as its proportion to the overall population, has increased in every census since then, rising to 14.1 million (6.2 percent) in 1980, 19.8 million (7.9 percent) in 1990, 31.1 million (11.1 percent) in 2000, and 40 million (12.9 percent) in 2010. That 2010 figure is the highest since 1920, when foreign-born people made up 13.2 percent of the population.

Some people today believe that legal immigration should be restricted again. These people maintain that immigrants take jobs native-born Americans could fill and that U.S. population growth, which immigration contributes to, harms the environment. Thus far, Congress has declined to place additional restrictions on immigration.

Today, the legal immigration system in the United States contains many rules, permitting only individuals who fit into certain categories to immigrate—and in many cases only after waiting anywhere from one to ten years or more, depending on the demand in that category. The system, representing a compromise among family, employment, and human rights concerns, has the following elements:

> A U.S. citizen may sponsor for immigration a spouse, parent, sibling, or minor or adult child.
>
> A lawful permanent resident (green card holder) may sponsor only a spouse or child.
>
> A foreign national may immigrate if he or she gains an employer sponsor.
>
> An individual who can show that he or she has a "well-founded fear of persecution" may come to the country as a refugee—or be allowed to stay as an asylee (someone who receives asylum).

Beyond these categories, essentially the only other way to immigrate is to apply for and receive one of the "diversity" visas, which are granted annually by lottery to those from "underrepresented" countries.

A Short History of Canadian Immigration

In the 1800s, immigration into Canada was largely unrestricted. Farmers and artisans from England and Ireland made up a significant portion of 19th-century immigrants. England's Parliament passed laws that facilitated and encouraged the voyage to North America, particularly for the poor.

After the United States barred Chinese railroad workers from settling in the country, Canada encouraged the immigration of Chinese laborers to assist in the building of Canadian railways. Responding to the racial views of the time, the Canadian Parliament began charging a "head tax" for Chinese and South Asian (Indian) immigrants in 1885. The fee of $50—later raised to $500—was well beyond the means of laborers making one or two dollars a day. Later, the government sought additional ways to prohibit Asians from entering the country. For example, it decided to require a "continuous journey," meaning that immigrants to Canada had to travel from their country on a boat that made an uninterrupted passage. For immigrants or asylum seekers from Asia this was nearly impossible.

As the 20th century progressed, concerns about race led to further restrictions on immigration to Canada. These restrictions particularly hurt Jewish and other refugees seeking to flee persecution in Europe. Government statistics indicate that Canada accepted no more than 5,000 Jewish refugees before and during the Holocaust.

After World War II, Canada, like the United States, began accepting thousands of Europeans displaced by the war. Canada's laws were modified to accept these war refugees, as well as Hungarians fleeing Communist authorities after the crushing of the 1956 Hungarian Revolution.

The Immigration Act of 1952 in Canada allowed for a "tap on, tap off" approach to immigration, granting administrative authorities the power to allow more immigrants into the country in good economic times, and fewer in times of recession. The shortcoming of such an approach is that there is little evidence

Early Indian Immigrants to Canada

Canada's first Indian immigrants were Sikhs, who arrived in 1904 to the cities of Victoria and Vancouver, located in the western province of British Columbia. They were attracted to the area after hearing tales from returning British Indian soldiers about the region's beauty and high wages. During the early 20th century, more Sikhs settled in British Columbia than anywhere else in Canada or the United States.

The Sikhs worked in logging camps and lumber mills. At that time all Canadians were legally British subjects, and as British citizens, Sikhs had the right to vote. According to Harold Coward, history professor at the University of Victoria, by 1908 about 5,000 Indians had arrived, most of them Sikhs. By that point the area's small white population had felt threatened by the Sikhs' numbers, and anti-immigration sentiment had grown considerably.

In 1908, British Columbia's legislature denied Asian immigrants voting and other rights. The same year Canada implemented the "continuous journey" law, which required South Asians to book passage on a ship traveling without stop from their country of origin. Because no ship line traveled continuously from India to Canada, legal immigration was impossible.

In defiance of the regulation, wealthy Sikh merchant Gurdt Singh Sarhali chartered a Japanese steamer, the *Komagata Maru*, and brought many Indian immigrants along for a journey departing from Hong Kong. When the ship arrived in Vancouver Harbor on May 23, 1914, with 376 Indians onboard, it received a hostile reception. Its passengers remained isolated for two months, while Canadian authorities refused to allow food and water to be brought aboard. Eventually, the passengers were deported, except for those few who had previously established residency in British Columbia.

Essentially cut off from their families, some of Canada's Indians returned to India or moved to the United States. In the 1920s, a few wives and children of those who remained in British Columbia were allowed to join them. The continuous journey regulation remained in effect until 1947, when it was removed along with the voting and other restrictions.

In 1999, Canada issued a postage stamp commemorating Sikh Canadian contributions to the country. It depicted a *khanda*, a double-edged sword representing divine knowledge. Revenue Minister Herb Dhaliwal, the first Indian appointed to a cabinet in a Western democracy, attended the unveiling. Dhaliwal's Sikh grandfather immigrated to Canada in 1906.

immigrants harm a national economy and much evidence they contribute to economic growth, particularly in the growth of the labor force.

In 1966 the government of Prime Minister Lester Pearson introduced a policy statement stressing how immigrants were key to Canada's economic growth. With Canada's relatively small population base, it became clear that in the absence of newcomers, the country would not be able to grow. The policy was introduced four years after Parliament enacted important legislation that eliminated Canada's own version of racially based national-origin quotas.

In 1967 a new law established a points system that awarded entry to potential immigrants using criteria based primarily on an individual's age, language ability, skills, education, family relationships, and job prospects. The total points needed for entry of an immigrant is set by the Minister of Citizenship and Immigration Canada. The new law also established a category for humanitarian (refugee) entry.

The 1976 Immigration Act refined and expanded the possibility for entry under the points system, particularly for those seeking to sponsor family members. The act also expanded refugee and asylum law to comport with Canada's international obligations. The law established five basic categories for immigration into Canada: 1) family; 2) humanitarian; 3) independents (including skilled workers), who immigrate to Canada on their own; 4) assisted relatives; and 5) business immigrants (including investors, entrepreneurs, and the self-employed).

The new Immigration and Refugee Protection Act, which took effect June 28, 2002, made a series of modifications to existing Canadian immigration law. The act, and the regulations that followed, toughened rules on those seeking asylum and the process for removing people unlawfully in Canada.

The law modified the points system, adding greater flexibility for skilled immigrants and temporary workers to become permanent residents, and evaluating skilled workers on the weight of their transferable skills as well as those of their specific occupation. The legislation also made it easier for employers to have a labor shortage declared in an industry or sector, which would facilitate the entry of foreign workers in that industry or sector.

On family immigration, the act permitted parents to sponsor dependent children up to the age of 22 (previously 19 was the maximum age at which a child could be sponsored for immigration). The act also allowed partners in common-law arrangements, including same-sex partners, to be considered as family members for the purpose of immigration sponsorship. Along with these liberalizing measures, the act also included provisions to address perceived gaps in immigration-law enforcement.

Indian Immigration to the United States

It is unknown exactly how many Indians entered the United States before 1950 because census records list them as "Others" or "Other Asians." Few immigrants from India came before 1965. With such a long distance between North America and South Asia, the United States was not the most popular destination, particularly for students. Wealthier Indians often studied abroad in England instead.

According to the census reports, from 1948 through 1965, approximately 6,474 Indians immigrated to the United States. In 1960, 391 out of 265,398 immigrants arriving to the country were from India. However, by 1965, there were 10,000 to 20,000 Indian immigrants living in America.

The 1960s brought many changes to the United States. By this point a very prosperous country, the United States broadened its international policy, becoming more involved in world affairs. Antiwar demonstrators protested the prolonged U.S. involvement in Vietnam. President Lyndon B. Johnson signed into law his Great Society social reform bills, which included measures on Medicare and other forms of federal aid. And Congress eliminated racially based admission policies by passing the Immigration Act of 1965.

The new immigration policy also would allow the United States to bring educated, skilled newcomers to its shores. The

U.S. space program, military contractors, universities, and aircraft companies hoped to attract scientists and engineers. Great Society medical programs required more doctors. When President Johnson signed the immigration bill in a ceremony at the Statue of Liberty on October 3, 1965, he stated that the new law "says simply that from this day forth those wishing to immigrate to America shall be admitted on the basis of their skills and their close relationship to those already here."

When the new law came into full effect in 1968, it removed barriers to Asian immigration. Also, travel to the United States was within the means of many since airfares were relatively inexpensive. As a result, large extended families of Asians began to arrive. According to INS reports, 27,189 Indians arrived during the 1960s, ready to begin a new life in America.

In the 1970s, American companies such as IBM and Xerox were hiring Indian engineers. Technicians, scientists, doctors, engineers, and scholars came as well. By 1980, Indian Americans numbered almost 400,000. Another quarter-million came during the 1980s. By 1990, there were more than 450,000 Indian immigrants living in the United States and more than 800,000 of Indian descent.

The 1990s hi-tech boom generated thousands of computer-related jobs that went unfilled. An estimated 1.6 million high-tech jobs were available in 2000. At the time, India was graduating 73,000 information technology professionals each year from 6 institutes of technology and 43 private and regional colleges. In the United States, some of these graduates were offered positions paying as much as 10 times what they would earn in India. Also, many Indians were hired by U.S. firms after completing graduate degrees at American universities.

From 1990 to 2000, the Indian immigrant population in the United States rose 124 percent, from 450,000 to 1 million, a higher increase than that of any other Asian country. In the 2000 Census, the total population of Indian Americans was about 1.7 million. That population has continued to grow. In 2013, according to data from the U.S. Census Bureau, the Indian

Illegal Immigration to the United States

Each year, approximately a million immigrants are legally admitted to the United States. But over the years the undocumented (illegal) portion of the U.S. population has increased. By 2016, the Pew Research Center estimates, approximately 11.3 million undocumented immigrants were living in the United States.

In recent years, the U.S. government has created programs that would help some of these undocumented immigrants to attain legal status within the United States. In June 2012, U.S. President Barack Obama announced a new government policy called Deferred Action for Childhood Arrivals (DACA). Persons who had entered the country illegally before the age of 16, who had lived in the country continuously since June 2007 (later changed to January 1, 2010), and who fulfilled certain other requirements could qualify under DACA, which protected them from being deported back to their parents' country of origin.

In November 2014, President Obama announced another policy, Deferred Action for Parents of Americans and Lawful Permanent Residents, or DAPA. Under DAPA, undocumented immigrants who had lived in the United States continuously since January 1, 2010, and who had children who were U.S. citizens or lawful permanent residents would be exempt from deportation. They could also receive a renewable three-year work permit. However, several states filed lawsuits over DAPA, and in February 2015 a federal court halted the implementation of DAPA pending the outcome of those suits.

In the meantime, the U.S. government has also taken many steps increase security on the borders and prevent illegal immigration. As of 2015, fences lined more than a third of the 1,989-mile (3,200-km) U.S.-Mexico land boundary. In 2015 the Department of Homeland Security requested nearly $13 billion for Customs and Border Protection. In 2002, by comparison, only $5 billion had been allocated for those functions. While there were slightly under 8,600 U.S. Border Patrol agents in 2000, by 2015 that number stood at about 21,000. Those agents patrol the border in trucks and helicopters, on horseback and quad bikes to prevent illegal crossings. In desert areas they may drag car tires to smooth the sand, making it easier to spot footprints. In other areas seismic sensors buried under roads or along well-traveled paths detect the sound of footsteps. Floodlights illuminate fences, and infrared cameras track movements of anyone trying to slip across the border in the darkness. Drones circle overhead constantly.

American population was about 3.1 million Americans.

Many Indian immigrants have been recruited on H-1B visas that have allowed them to work and live in the United States for up to six years. The purpose of H-1B visas is to bring foreign workers to the United States to fill jobs when there are not enough American workers qualified for those jobs. Often, these jobs are in specialized fields such as computer technology or engineering. Many immigrants who enter on H-1B visas apply for a green card, which allows them to stay permanently.

According to statistics from U.S. Citizenship and Immigration Services, in 2014 Indians made up about 70 percent of the petitions for H-1B visas that were approved in 2014. The top H-1B employers that year included several Indian multinational companies with operations in the United States, as well as consulting firms like Accenture and Deloitte and American tech firms like IBM, Microsoft, and Syntel.

Employers hiring more than 15 percent of their workers on H-1B visas are considered "H-1B dependent." Before they can hire more foreigners, they must prove they tried to hire American workers first, but could not find qualified job applicants.

Indian Immigration to Canada

In 1951, annual immigration from India to Canada averaged 150 people per year. Most who came were relatives of Sikhs who settled in the country during the early 1900s. In the 1960s immigration increased from parts of India other than Punjab, where Sikhs comprise the majority.

The first wave of South Asian immigrants in the 1960s consisted of well-educated, upper-middle-class teachers, engineers, doctors, and other professionals who spoke fluent English. Many taught in Canada's universities. A large group of Hindus came from Uttar Pradesh and nearby regions in northern India. Some Tamil Hindus from Madras (a former Indian state that was re-named Tamil Nadu) came as teachers. Throughout the 1970s and 1980s waves of Indians, other Asian immigrants, and people from Africa, the Caribbean, and Latin America arrived to Canada.

Some Indians came as refugees from Africa. When Ugandan president Idi Amin expelled tens of thousands of Indian investors and gave their property to Africans in 1972, Canada accepted 7,000 Indians as political refugees. According to a Migration Information Source report, from 1956 to 1976, 63.6 percent of

Canada's immigrants came from the United Kingdom and Europe, while only 11.9 percent came from Asia. By 2000, the totals from these regions had completely changed: 18.9 percent were coming from the United Kingdom and Europe, and 53 percent from Asia. More than half of Canada's South Asians was from India. By 2014, India ranked second as a source country of immigrants to Canada, behind only the Philippines.

 Text-Dependent Questions

1. Name the U.S. law that prevented most Asian immigrants from entering the country. When did the law go into effect? When was it repealed?
2. What steps did the Canadian government take to limit immigration before the 1960s?
3. Why did many Indian workers come to the United States during the 1990s?

 Research Project

Investigate the contribution of Asian laborers to the construction of the Transcontinental Railroad. Write a two-page report.

4 Making a New Life

Indian immigrants to North America make many sacrifices. They leave a home where they knew most or all of their neighbors and arrive in a place where they may know no one at all. Middle-class immigrants may give up having servants to do their cooking, cleaning, and gardening, and their new jobs may mean lower status even though they may receive higher pay. Some immigrants who have advanced degrees but lack Canadian or American professional licenses must first accept menial jobs. Like all immigrants, the dream of a better life for them and their families remains their inspiration during difficult times.

Settling In

Most immigrants are motivated to work hard and succeed. They are adventurous enough to strike out on their own to a place hundreds—or even thousands—of miles from home. Often their strong sense of family and community helps them succeed. Relatives may lend them money to buy or start a business. Older relatives in the household may help with housework and childcare, freeing up parents to work long hours. Immigrants who have built successful businesses may hire new arrivals from their country.

◀A Sikh American taxi driver picks up a passenger in New York. Taxi driving is one of the many trades that Indian Americans have entered in the United States. In New York City, an estimated 70 percent of the cab drivers hail from the South Asian countries of India, Pakistan, and Bangladesh.

When immigrants arrive to the United States, they are often surprised to find that life is not like what they have seen in Hollywood movies. Some are surprised by the cultural diversity or by the fact that most people live in ordinary homes instead of mansions. Customs and slang may confuse even the well educated.

Most Indian arrivals at least have the advantage of speaking English and having some familiarity with Western-style institutions. But even when a job is waiting for them, they must first find housing and transportation and open a bank account. Some employers arrange temporary housing and transportation for foreign employees, or they pair the new hire with a mentor. Family members who are already settled may also help immigrants get started in their new lives.

Immigrant parents hope for a better education and more opportunities for their children than they had. They expect their children to excel in school, and usually they do excel. A report of the Children of Immigrants Longitudinal Study conducted in Southern California found that second-generation Indian high school students ranked second only to Chinese students among immigrant groups in terms of high grade averages and low dropout rates.

Indians settle in big cities, suburbs, and small towns, often near universities, hospitals, or high-tech corporations. The highest concentrations of Indian Americans live in California, New York, New Jersey, Texas, and Illinois. There are more than 525,000 Indian Americans in California, over 300,000 in New

 Words to Understand in This Chapter

Bollywood—a thriving film industry based in India.
diaspora—the scattering of people who live outside their native country.
sari—a traditional woman's garment consisting of nearly seven yards of fabric wrapped around the body.

New York Mayor Bill DeBlasio leads the annual Indian Day Parade along Madison Avenue. The parade marks the anniversary of India's independence.

York and New Jersey, about 250,000 in Texas, and nearly 200,000 in Illinois. According to U.S. Census Bureau data, Florida, Virginia, Pennsylvania, and Georgia are all home to more than 100,000 Indian Americans.

Many Indian immigrants have settled in the metropolitan areas of New York and northern New Jersey, such as Newark and Jersey City. This area has a number of predominantly Indian neighborhoods that have each become known as Little India. Other thriving Indian communities exist in San Francisco, California; Miami and Tampa Bay, Florida; Chicago, Illinois. Seattle, Washington; Los Angeles and the San Jose–Palo Alto region (Silicon Valley) of California; and Detroit, Michigan.

Indian Settlement in Major U.S. Cities

Traditionally a gateway for newly arrived foreigners, New York City has drawn more immigrants than any other American city.

Indian restaurants line the streets of the Little India section of New York's Greenwich Village. Another Little India has sprung up in the Queens borough of New York, and similar neighborhoods are found in major cities like Toronto, San Fransisco, and Miami.

Many Indian Americans living in New York City hail from the cities of Mumbai and Gujarat. Newcomers and first- and second-generation immigrants alike enjoy the proximity of Indian restaurants and groceries, mosques, and Hindu temples. Indian immigrants have established a niche in some job fields, paving the way for other newcomers. A popular job among Indians living in New York is driving taxis: the Taxi and Limousine Commission of New York City estimated that about 70 percent of the city's cab drivers are immigrants from India, Pakistan, and Bangladesh.

The greater metropolitan area of New York also attracts Indian immigrants. Beginning in the 1990s, a large number of Indian newcomers started to settle in the borough of Queens, mostly in the Jackson Heights neighborhood. There merchants established a "Little India" shopping area and organized to deal with civic issues. Today some Indian Americans are moving farther beyond the city. The Indian American population in upscale Westchester County has grown significantly since 1980.

An estimated 150,000 Indian Americans, many from Gujarat, live in northern California. The San Francisco Bay Area Federation of Indo-American Associations organizes events such as an Independence Day celebration, complete with parades, concerts, and visiting **Bollywood** film stars. At Thanksgiving, Bay Area Indian Americans feed San Jose's homeless and distribute winter blankets.

Over the years, the northside of Chicago and its nearby suburbs attracted many Indian doctors, engineers, and scientists,

Helping Two Communities

Known around Tampa, Florida, as "Dr. K," cardiologist Kiran C. Patel has given back much to his native and adopted countries. Patel was born in the African country of Zambia but grew up in Gujarat, India. His father, an accountant, pushed him hard in his academic studies. "My father said that if I were second in my class, I should not even bother to put my foot in the house," Patel told the *Tampa Tribune*.

After graduating from Cambridge University and the University of London in England, Patel completed his medical degree at Gujarat University in 1974. He moved to the United States in 1976 after completing residencies in India and Zambia. Patel received additional medical training at Jersey City Medical Center before accepting a fellowship at Columbia University in New York City.

In 1982 Patel started his practice in Tampa. Two years later, with one employee, he founded a physician practice management company. In 1992, he bought Well Care, a small HMO, which he eventually built up into Florida's largest Medicaid provider—a $1-billion business employing 1,200. In July 2002, he sold Well Care to New York investors for an undisclosed sum.

Dr. K and his wife, pediatrician Dr. Pallavi Patel, have shared a great deal of their accumulated wealth. They were instrumental in establishing the India Cultural Center in Tampa, and started a college scholarship fund for underprivileged students. They also helped fund the construction of a modern 50-bed hospital and school in Gujarat. In October 2002, Dr. Patel donated $5 million to the Tampa Bay Performing Arts Center. Chairman of Visionary Medical Systems, a medical software company, Dr. Patel also has served as president of the American Association of Physicians of Indian Origin.

This Hindu temple is located in Chicago, where there is a thriving Indian American community.

who later sponsored their relatives to emigrate to the United States. The Chicago area today is home to some 171,000 Indian Americans, according to the 2010 U.S. Census.

In the 1970s, Indian immigrants began to establish businesses in a Chicago neighborhood along Devon Avenue, opening grocery stores, restaurants, video and gift shops, and stores selling Indian jewelry and *saris* (a traditional dress worn by Indian women). Ultimately the neighborhood became known as Indiatown, recognized as a major marketplace of Indian goods and services.

During the 1980s, an economic recession increased the need for social services in Chicago. Nearly 18 percent of the city's Indian population was reported to live below the poverty level. In order to provide health and family services for Chicago's Indian population, activists founded the nonprofit Indo-American Center in 1996, and set up the organization's headquarters in the former Jewish Community Center building. At the center immigrants can take literacy and civics classes, as well as receive help filling out application forms to become U.S. citizens. Chicago-area temples and mosques take part in feeding the homeless and other charitable activities.

Southern and Midwestern Communities

The 2010 U.S. Census reported that Georgia's Indian community had increased by 108 percent during the previous decade, and today Indian Americans are the state's largest Asian group. As of 2016, there were about 100,000 Indian Americans residing in Georgia, with approximately 80,000 living in the Atlanta area. Initially, many Indian graduate students came to the area to attend the universities; immigrants arriving later came for high-tech jobs located in Atlanta and other cities. Indian Festivals at Atlanta's Civic Center feature pageants, folk music and dances, seminars, workshops, food, and arts and crafts.

The area around Washington, D.C.—which includes Arlington and Alexandria, Virginia—was home to about 130,000 Indian Americans in 2016, according to the Census Bureau. In California, the Los Angeles, San Francisco, and San Jose areas were each home to about 120,000 Indian Americans. The Dallas-Fort Worth metropolitan area was home to an Indian American community of more than 100,000.

One of the oldest Indian American communities is located in Cleveland, Ohio. It was started by a group of Indians—mainly composed of university students—who started migrating there during the 1920s. According to census reports, the community grew from 100 in the 1930s to 5,780 in 1990. Today, it numbers roughly 15,000 people. Most of the immigrants came from Gujarat. Later arrivals included a greater number of doctors, engineers, and other professionals. The newcomers first settled close to hospitals and colleges on the city's east side. In the 1970s immigrants and first- and second-generation Indians began settling farther away from the city in the western suburbs.

In December 1962, when India was in the midst of a five-year-old border conflict with China, a small assembly of 100 people attended a meeting in Cleveland to discuss the recent Chinese invasion of India. By 1964 that group had evolved into the India Association of Cleveland. The creation of other organizations followed, including the India Community Center. Established in 1976, the center offered courses in Indian cooking, languages, dance, and music. The center also showed documentaries about India, operated a speaker's bureau, and published *The Lotus*, a free monthly newspaper for the Indian community. This organization remains active in Indian American affairs today, though it has been renamed the Federation of India Community Associations of Northeast Ohio.

Many of the Indians who arrived to St. Louis in the mid-1960s were college and medical students. Many of these students stayed after completing their degrees, helping establish an Indian community that continued to thrive during the 1990s, when the local information technology industry provided numerous jobs. Indians and Indian Americans were employed as doctors, chemists, scientists, programmers, and professors. Those who owned businesses ran liquor stores, markets, and Indian restaurants.

The Indian community of St. Louis, reported to number 17,000 people in 2016, continues to thrive today. Some companies specialize in meeting the particular needs of the community: Seema Enterprises and Shriji Enterprises run travel agencies and stores that sell Indian foods, CDs, books, and movies. The Mahatma Gandhi Center, next door to the Hindu temple, offers cultural programs such as demonstrations by traditional dance troupes. In 1997, the India Association of St. Louis sponsored a festival celebrating the 50th anniversary of India's independence from Great Britain.

Indian Communities in Canada

In Canada, most Indians settle in the largest cities—Toronto, Vancouver, Calgary, Montreal, and Edmonton. The largest Asian Indian community is located in Toronto, which is also the most

Canadians take part in the Festival of India parade in Toronto.

ethnically diverse city in the country. It is 60 percent nonwhite and home to 110 ethnic groups and languages. About 575,000 Asian Indians live in Toronto. Another 217,000 live in Vancouver and 66,000 in Calgary. Montreal and Edmonton each have Asian Indians communities of about 46,000. Canada's cities tend to be densely populated and culturally diverse, while rural Canada remains sparsely populated.

In Toronto's Little India, food stand owners sell Indian treats such as grilled corn on the cob, fruit juices, fresh-squeezed sugarcane, and *kulfi* (Indian ice cream). The neighborhood also has restaurants, grocers, jewelers, and shops selling music CDs, videos, and saris.

Vancouver hosts a large Sikh population, many of whom are descendants of the first pioneer immigrants who came in the early part of the 20th century. The Khalsa Diwan Society, established in 1906, oversees community needs and sponsors Sikh festivals and parades. Vancouver's East Indian shops along Main Street sell spices and other Indian groceries, gold bangles, religious icons, fabric, and saris. Restaurants serve authentic Indian foods. North America's first Sikh school, Khalsa Elementary, is located near Vancouver's shopping district.

Occupations

A large number of Indians continue to come to North America as students. Many who graduate become professionals and work in the U.S. as doctors, lawyers, scientists, professors, engineers, and computer programmers. They may run Fortune 500 companies and start their own companies. Thousands of Indian Americans have become millionaires in high-tech enterprises, and more than half a dozen have become billionaires.

Immigrant entrepreneurs frequently start businesses that cater to the needs of other immigrants. Shops sell Indian groceries, saris, jewelry, and DVDs of Bollywood movies and Indian television programs. A recent business that is thriving in the immigrant community, especially in New York City, is the sale of prepaid long-distance phone cards to other immigrants who call home frequently. Suppliers are Indian-owned companies that buy leftover time from major carriers and then resell the minutes through phone cards.

Authentic Indian restaurants are popular in North America, but starting up such businesses can pose challenges. Owners must obtain financing and sometimes import necessary cooking equipment, food, and spices, and must hire a qualified chef who is a legal resident. Also, in keeping with the tradition of Indian restaurants, they often must provide staff with a salary and free room.

Other Indian immigrants drive limousines or taxis, or operate stationery stores or self-service laundries. Some Indian entrepreneurs have contracted to run newspaper kiosks in New York's subways. In south and central New Jersey, Indians dominate the motel business.

Cultural Organizations

Worldwide, the Indian *diaspora*—the collective group living outside India—includes approximately 25 million people. In North America, many Indians have found the need to form associations to explore their common interests. The oldest national Indian American organization, the Association of Indians in America (AIA), was founded in August 1967 and incorporated in 1971. Because so few Indians lived in the United States at the time, early organizations represented the interests of all. AIA focused on unity through its focus on Indian heritage. A similar organization, the India Canada Association, was also founded with the

One high-profile Indian-American politician is Bobby Jindal, who served as governor of Louisiana from 2008 to 2016. Jindal's parents had emigrated to the United States shortly before he was born.

Making a New Life 69

objective to promote social, cultural, and educational interests.

Around the time the AIA was established, several social student organizations were founded that brought Indian music, dance, and movies to those far from home. After the students of these groups graduated, many coordinated with other young Indian professionals to found organizations that championed more service-oriented goals. The groups met to discuss issues of common interest or help with development projects in India.

In the late summer of 1989, more than 3,000 Indian expatriates met in New York City to discuss common concerns and problems. As a result, the Global Organization of People of Indian Origin formed, with the goal to promote interests, cultural heritage, and interaction between Indian communities. Among the activities offered were workshops for entrepreneurs.

One of the largest Indian professional groups is the American Association of Physicians of Indian Origin. It claims a membership of 35,000 physicians and 10,000 medical students and residents.

In the hospitality industry, a popular field of investment for Indian entrepreneurs, Indians have formed advocacy groups to combat discrimination. In 1985, Midsouth Indemnity Association, which later became the National Indo-American Hospitality Association, formed in Tennessee. The Asian American Hotel Owners Association formed in Atlanta in 1989. In 1994 the two groups merged to become the Atlanta-based Asian American Hotel Owners Association.

Membership in the Asian American Hotel Owners Association (AAHOA) grew from fewer than 300 in 1989 to more than 15,000 by 2016. Its members today own more than 20,000 hotel or other properties, which comprise more than 40 percent of all hotels in the United States. AAHOA members employ over 600,000 American workers, and account for nearly $10 billion in payroll annually.

Perhaps the most well-known Indian professional group, IndUS Entrepreneurs (TiE), was established in 1992 to help new immigrants overcome obstacles. The founding members, high-tech executives and businesspeople from India and neighboring countries, provided mentoring, advice to streamline ideas, and free legal and accounting services. Members back startup companies and help them find skilled tech workers. Monthly meetings feature expert speakers and networking opportunities. IndUS Entrepreneurs operates ten chapters in the United States and five in India. Today, TiE has become an international organization, with 61 chapters in 18 countries and a membership of over 12,000.

In addition to the scores of professional organizations, groups have also formed to serve the religious and cultural interests of Indian immigrants. Members of these groups hope to pass their heritage and history to future generations. Hundreds of these local groups, many specialized according to religion, region, or language, operate throughout North America.

 Text-Dependent Questions

1. In what U.S. state is the largest group of Indian Americans found?
2. What city in Ohio is home to one of the oldest Indian American communities?
3. Which Canadian city is home to the largest Asian Indian community?

 Research Project

If your family is Indian and you speak an Indian language, write a few sentences in that language and translate them into English. If you're not Indian, use the Internet to learn how to say four or five basic phrases (such as *hello, thank you*, and *goodbye*) in Hindi or another Indian language.

5 Keeping the Culture Alive

Just as a new student in school wants to feel comfortable, make friends, and succeed, a foreigner in a new country wants to build a life and become comfortable in that new environment. He or she may choose to dress and act like the native people while at the same time aiming to preserve the culture and heritage of the homeland.

People have a multitude of different ideas about what it means to be American, Canadian, Indian, or a mixture of these nationalities. Indians living in North America typically distinguish among themselves those who are American- or Canadian-born, or at least longtime residents, and those who are newly arrived, are not yet English-speaking, and wear native dress. *Assimilation* is the process by which an immigrant becomes part of mainstream society. Using slang or wearing Western fashions are just a few examples of assimilation.

The Faiths of Indian Immigrants

Indian immigrants who came to North America before the 1960s tried to fit in more than stand out, an approach that was

◀ An Indian Sikh market owner, wearing a turban as a symbol of his faith, displays his merchandise in Vancouver, Canada. Many immigrants practicing the various religions of the homeland strive to maintain their customs and tenets.

not always easy in countries where few women wore saris or *bindis*. Today most Indian immigrants carry on their country's heritage by following the religion they practiced in India. Among these various faiths are Hinduism, Islam, Jainism, Parsism, and Sikhism.

Part of Indian culture for 5,000 years, Hinduism is one of the world's oldest religions. Owing to the multitude of Hindu sects, specific beliefs vary throughout India. Much of the religion is preserved through dedication to rituals and ceremony. Most Hindus accept the caste system and consider the Vedas the most sacred of the ancient scriptures. Hindus also believe that Karma, a force of destiny, propels living beings through a cycle of birth and rebirth. All Hindu gods, such as Rama, Krishna, Shiva, and the elephant-headed god Ganesha, are considered forms of one Supreme Being.

The earliest Hindu immigrants prayed in makeshift facilities ranging from mattress showrooms to YMCA buildings. After the establishment of the Hindu Temple Society of North America in 1970, the organization built one of North America's first Hindu temples in Flushing, New York. While Hindu temples in India are open shrines designed for individual prayer, North American temples are constructed to accommodate group worship. To suit working schedules, temples hold events on Sundays, which is not done in India. Just as classical Indian dancers might perform at

Words to Understand in This Chapter

ashimsa—a deep religious reverence for life, with extreme avoidance of injuring living things.
assimilation—the process of adopting characteristics of and being absorbed into a new culture.
bindi—a distinctive round red dot in the center of the forehead, usually signifying marriage in India.
Diwali—Festival of Lights celebrating the victory of good over evil and the beginning of the new year.
mela—a large social gathering or a feast of Indian foods.
rangoli—art from natural materials such as rice, flower petals, or tinted rice flour.

Hindu deities are paraded through the streets of Toronto as part of a festival.

a Catholic mass in India, American Hindu worship often exhibits an American influence.

Islam is the second most popular faith among Indian immigrants. The word *Islam* comes from the Arabic verb *aslama*, which roughly means "to gain peace by submitting to the will of God." The religion is based on the teachings of Muhammad, born in Mecca in 570 CE. His revelations concerning the oneness of God, Allah, and the folly of worshipping idols are written in the Qur'an, the sacred text of Islam. Islam defines a distinct way of behavior for a universal community worshipping one God. In contrast, Hinduism is also a distinct way of life, yet recognizes many gods and asserts inequalities between people. Many Muslims in India follow a doctrine that has been long integrated into Indian culture.

One of the first meeting places in North America for Muslims was the Islamic Center in Michigan City, Indiana, built in the early 1900s. For many years most Muslims lacked access to mosques and met for worship in rented halls or cafes. Today, there are temples and mosques throughout Canada and the United States.

Jainism originated in India, where Jains make up class of wealthy professionals. They are followers of Mahavira, a prince

The Hare Krishna Movement

An offshoot of Hinduism, the New York City–based Hare Krishna movement attracted many young followers during the 1960s. Sporting shaved heads and saffron color robes, they danced, chanted, beat drums, and jingled bells on the streets, asking for change. A. C. Bhaktivedanta Swami Prabhupada founded the movement in Calcutta in 1896 and brought it to New York in 1965.

Hare Krishnas follow the holy book Bhagavad-Gita and believe the Hindu god Krishna took human form to save mankind from a materialistic existence. The International Society for Krishna Consciousness was founded in Great Britain in 1968, and George Harrison of the rock band the Beatles became its most famous devotee. Hare Krishna's Food for Life Program operates free restaurants, homeless shelters, and provides emergency relief in 60 countries.

Hare Krishna followers recite their mantra in a New York park.

Portrait of a Sikh family wearing traditional clothing. There are believed to be about 500,000 followers of the Sikh religion in the United States, and a similar number in Canada.

in northeast India who reigned during the fifth century BCE. Appalled by the region's poverty, Mahavira sought to reform the Hindu caste system that helped create the poor conditions of his people.

Jains believe in reincarnation, nonviolence, and respect for the environment. They practice meditation and self-denial, believing that desire causes suffering and that the good life is attained only through deprivation. As strict vegetarians, their reverence for life runs so deep they avoid even accidentally stepping on an insect. They respect other viewpoints and live by the "Three Jewels" of right conduct, right knowledge, and right worldview.

To preserve their religion against the spread of Islam, the Parsis from ancient Persia fled Iran more than 1,000 years ago. The king of Gujarat offered them refuge, and they lived peacefully with the Hindus. Followers of the Iranian prophet

Keeping the Culture Alive

Traditional attire for Indian women includes a sari and a *dupatta* (a scarf draped over the shoulder). A more complete outfit will add a jacket and *salwar* (pants).

Zoroaster, they adhere to the three virtues of "good thoughts, good words, good deeds." Fairer skinned and taller than most Indians, they are the most Westernized of India's ethnic groups.

Based mainly in Mumbai, the Parsis are mainly middle class and well educated. Originally farmers and artisans, under British rule the Parsis built most of India's industry and amassed fortunes. Some changed their last names to fit their occupations, frequently tacking on the suffix *-wala*, meaning "dealer" or "manufacturer." This resulted in intriguing Parsi surnames such as Printer, Readymoney, and Sodabottleopenerwala.

The Sikh religion was founded in the 15th century in Punjab, a lush northwestern agricultural region. It is founded primarily on the teachings of 10 gurus. The first guru, Nanak, was enlightened by God's message after he disappeared for three days in the Bain River. Three hundred years after Nanak was first enlightened, the 10th guru, Gobind Singh, declared the principles of the faith: sacrifice, chastity, courage, service, and struggle against injustice. Sikh followers are required to wear certain symbols of faith, including a turban, dagger, combs, and bracelets. They reject the caste system and consider it their duty to help make the world a better place.

Although Buddhism originated in India, only a small group of Buddhists, mainly refugees from China and converted lower caste Hindus, lives there today. Founded in 525 BCE by Siddhartha Gautama—the Buddha—Buddhism thrived throughout India until the 13th century. A revival of Hinduism and invasions by Huns and Muslims contributed to its decline. Buddhists believe in reincarnation, or a cycle of birth and rebirth. They stress the importance of meditation and follow basic moral rules.

Traditional Clothing and Food

Most Indian women in North America wear Western clothing except on special occasions. Today's Indian designers create both traditional styles and Westernized modern designs. A sari is worn with a *dupatta* (a scarf draped over the shoulder), and a *lehanga* is a jacket, flared skirt, and dupatta. A *salwar lehanga* combines the jacket, skirt, and *dupatta* with *salwar* (pants). Many Indian women wear a pantsuit known as a *churidaar*. The pants are tight at the bottom with fabric draped over the ankles to resemble bangles. A top called a *kameez* is worn over the pants and is worn with a dupatta.

Up until the end of the 1960s, there were few Indian stores in North America, so immigrants would ask their relatives to purchase saris and traditional jewelry when they visited India. In return, they supplied Western items to relatives living in India.

During the period when there was a lack of Indian restaurants and Indian grocery stores, even in the major cities, Indian immigrants struggled to maintain a similar diet to what they had in their homeland. The central problem was that many Indians are vegetarian, and there were few shopping opportunities for them. The vegetarian practice originated in India, where many people seriously follow the religious ethic of being in harmony with creation. Three of the country's major religions—Hinduism, Jainism, and Buddhism—believe in *ashimsa* (nonviolence), a principle that applies to the treatment of all living things, including animals. However, some Indians who were vegetarian in their native countries began eating meat after emigrating.

Before the 1970s, mainstream restaurants did not offer vegetarian menu selections. Indian cooking ingredients were not available, so some immigrants improvised with what was available to them. Relatives also mailed spices from India, or immigrants brought them back from a visit to the country. Makeshift homemade Indian cuisine was often served at weekend social gatherings.

Enterprising immigrants decided to meet the needs of their community. In 1970, Gorthandas Soni and his brother opened House of Spices in Flushing, New York, and began to provide high-quality imported Indian food. Today the company operates retail stores throughout the United States, selling grains, specialty rice, spices, pickles, chutney, and Indian sweets and snacks. It also manufactures its own food products.

Today, Indian Americans can go to a local supermarket to obtain almost any food they would find in India, thanks in part to a growing interest in vegetarianism and the popularity of Indian cuisine. Vegetarian offerings include salad bars, soybean meat imitations, veggie burgers and pizzas, vegetarian restaurants, and meatless pet foods. Taj brand frozen entrées include a variety of Indian vegetarian dinners with organic rice and vegetables. Gourmet ethnic foods can also be ordered off the Internet.

Preserving Indian Heritage

Many recent immigrants consider themselves Americans or Canadians who are keeping alive their Indian culture. They use dance performances, music, literature, movies, art exhibitions, cultural workshops, religious rituals, and festivals to preserve their Indian heritage. For example, in 1996 an organization called the Asian Indian Historical Archive Committee recorded the experiences and perspectives of 12 of its members by producing a video documentary that filmed daily life in their Ohio homes.

First- and second-generation Indian writers have recorded their experiences through acclaimed poetry and fiction. In 1977, American-born novelist Clark Blaise and his wife, novelist Bharati Mukherjee, published a joint autobiographical account of their year in her native India called *Days and Nights in Calcutta*. G. S. Sharat Chandra's 1998 short story collection, *Sari of the Gods*, deals with Indian immigrants in North America.

The 2014 film *Million Dollar Arm* was based on a true story about a sports agent who tries to find talented baseball players in India and bring them to the United States.

Following a Dream

Rachna Gilmore grew up in an upper-middle-class family who lived in a Georgian mansion in Mumbai. When she was young girl, she first heard of her future home country, Canada, listening to her fourth-grade teacher read the novel *Anne of Green Gables* to the class.

Originally planning to study medicine, Gilmore received a bachelor's of science in 1974 from King's College in London. Afterward, she decided to travel, ultimately moving to Prince Edward Island, Canada, where she married and earned a bachelor's degree in elementary education.

In Canada, Gilmore worked as a paralegal researcher, then set up a pottery studio in her basement. After her two daughters were born in 1980 and 1984, the family moved to Ottawa. There, at age 30, Gilmore began to pursue her dream of writing.

Her first picture book, *My Mother is Weird*, was published in 1986. Her second children's book, *Wheniwasalittlegirl*, followed close behind. Under the pseudonym Rachna Mara, she published an adult short story collection entitled *Of Custom and Excise* in 1991. Gleaning material from her Indian background, she wrote *Lights for Gita*, the first in a Gita series that also includes *Roses for Gita* and *A Gift for Gita*. Her young-adult novel, *A Group of One*, written with a grant from the Department of Canadian Heritage, tells the story of a grandmother from India who visits her Westernized immigrant family in Ottawa.

Festivals, Parades, and Dance Performances

Diwali, the Festival of Lights, triggers a deep nostalgia for most Indians. Originally an ancient harvest celebration, it was later incorporated into the Hindu calendar of holidays and became a celebration of the new year. The holiday occurs in the Hindu month of Ashvin, which falls in October or November. Diwali celebrates the triumph of good over evil, commemorating Lord Rama's return to his birthplace after slaying Ravana, a 10-headed demon king. Diwali also marks the victory of Krishna, the celestial cowherd, over the demon Narakasura.

The events of Diwali begin 10 days or more in advance. The home is cleaned and decorated. Abstract *rangoli* designs made of natural materials such as rice, flower petals, or tinted rice flour adorn the entrance. They are then destroyed the first time a person walks through the door. Special foods are prepared, and Indians wear new clothes and exchange multicolor sweets with friends, neighbors, and business associates. During Diwali season, the House of Spices' Shamiana candy division works around the clock to produce 2,000 to 3,000 pounds of Indian sweets per day.

In India, Hindus observe Diwali by lighting thousands of clay oil lamps and candles and setting them on balconies and window ledges. They are placed there to welcome and light the way for Laksmi, the Hindu goddess of wealth, and Genesh, the god of good fortune and wisdom. Street musicians play and firecrackers, cherry bombs, and bottle rockets explode everywhere. The lighting of roman candles is a way to express joy, and is also believed to scare away evil spirits.

Many immigrants may take their children to visit India during the Diwali celebrations, or they may try to re-create them for their children, though in an entirely different form. Because it is a public holiday in India, Diwali may fall on a workday in North America, and in some communities fireworks are banned. In her book *Lights for Gita*, author Rachna Gilmore tells the story of an immigrant family celebrating Diwali in America for the first time. The title character experiences a quiet celebration on a

A crowd of people watches as an India Day parade passes through an Indian American neighborhood in Edison, New Jersey.

dark wintry night, in contrast to the excitement of New Delhi's public festival ablaze with fireworks, celebrated in the company of extended family.

In some Indian American communities, Diwali celebrations are nearly as elaborate as those in India. Festivities include street fairs, balls, luncheons, parades, dance parties, and fireworks displays. Along Chicago's Devon Avenue, colored lights from the Diwali festival are sometimes mistaken for Christmas decorations. The San Francisco Bay area's first Diwali *Mela* in 1994 combined festivities with fund-raising for a temple. Hundreds of lights sparkle along Jackson Heights' 74th Street in New York for the annual Diwali street fair, attended by more than 10,000 people.

Another significant holiday for Indians worldwide is celebrated on August 15, the date that India gained its independence from British colonial rule in 1947. Many North American cities

Indian immigrants to the U.S. and Canada often enjoy the films of Bollywood stars like Aishwarya Rai.

hold Independence Day parades. In Chicago, the local Federation of Indian Associations and large corporations sponsor the event. Indian movie stars, beauty queens, and political figures serve as the grand marshal and guests of honor.

In October or November, the Hindu festival Navaratri Mahotsav, or "Festival of Nine Nights," recognize another victory of good over evil. According to legend, the goddess Durga appeared to kill an evil spirit that could not be slain by any male. Especially popular in western India, Navratri celebrations vary from region to region. In Gujarat, a giant statue symbolizing evil is burned on the 10th day of the celebration. In North America, local universities and Indian associations sponsor Navratri festivals.

Other local festivals promote Indian culture. The India Association of Long Island organizes New York's Indiafest, which features Indian foods and stalls selling traditional clothing and Indian CDs. Local dance troupes perform traditional dances.

All Indian dance genres stem from the 2,000-year-old Natya Shastras (Theatre Scriptures) that portray scenes from Hindu mythology. The various Indian classical dance forms require years of practice and discipline. Most dancers specialize in one form. The performances of many Indian folk dances have become competitive events. *Bhangra*, a Punjabi folk dance and musical style, has become so popular that George Washington University, in Washington, D.C., sponsors an annual intercollegiate competition called the Bhangra Blowout. The Federation of Gujarati Association in North America organizes the North American Raas, a *garba* and folk-dance competition held in Newark, New Jersey. Miss India Worldwide organizes "Miss India U.S." and "Miss India Canada" beauty pageants in which contestants, mainly second-generation Indians, perform classical and folk dances.

Indian music has also found many Western listeners. The late 1980s brought a revival of ancient traditional Gandharva Veda melodies, which are believed to generate tranquility and energy. The "new Bhangra beat" features Indopop performers such as Bally Saghoo, Nitin Sawhney, and Cornershop.

Links Back Home

Some immigrants acknowledge the importance of connections with the homeland and make periodic visits to extended family members in India. Even by plane, the trip is long and expensive. For most Indian immigrants, it is difficult to visit frequently.

Those who cannot make the trip explore the various ways to stay in touch. For the early waves of immigrants, calls back home were expensive, requiring operators and often resulting in poor connections. Calls had to be coordinated to compensate for the 9- to 12-hour time difference between North America and India. Now Indian immigrants can connect with family and friends using less-expensive faxes and e-mails. Internet sites host cyber communities with news and chat rooms for dispersed Indians.

Most Indian organizations have websites for members and other people to stay connected.

Owing to the international success of Bollywood, India's thriving film industry, immigrants can keep track of the most recent movie sensations. Bollywood grew from the success of a three-hour epic called *Mother India*, first shown in 1957. Indian cinema has since gained worldwide popularity, though the early immigrants seldom had the opportunity to see Indian films. Today, immigrants can remain up-to-date on all the latest movies and music produced in India. Satellite television stations broadcast Indian TV shows and movies. Some movie theaters show nothing but Indian movies, while video and CD shops sell recordings of movies and Hindi songs from soundtracks.

Changing Generations

First-generation Indian immigrants face many tasks to establish their new lives. They must deal with obtaining legal status, settling into a home, and achieving financial security. Many keep their own company and seldom venture out of the immediate community. Some feel that they are too busy to maintain their religious traditions.

The second generation—the children of Indian immigrants—may share their parents' values but from a different viewpoint. Frequently, they feel more comfortable in Western society and are accustomed to enjoying more freedoms. Like many young people, the children of Indian immigrants see their parents as too conservative. In turn, their parents worry that their sons and daughters will become too materialistic or too Westernized and lose their religious identity and culture.

The children of Indian immigrants may clash with their parents over permission to participate in activities unfamiliar to them, such as coed parties or proms. Many parents allow their children to eventually find their own partners rather than arrange marriages for them, but they maintain hope that their sons and daughters will marry within their own culture.

As settled as Indian immigrants may become in their new

country, many never stop yearning for their first home. Author Jhumpa Lahiri, a second-generation immigrant, said in a 1999 *Newsweek International* interview, "I've inherited my parents' preoccupations. It's hard to have parents who consider another place 'home'—even after living abroad for 30 years, India is home for them."

Some Indian immigrants arrive in the United States or Canada expecting to stay just long enough to save a satisfactory amount of money for a comfortable retirement and then return home. However, not all who plan to return do so. After living many years abroad, they lose the connection with their homeland or the decision to return becomes impractical.

When the Internet was launched in India in 1996, many enterprising computer professionals were presented with new opportunities. Some who had been working in North America raised enough money to start up technology companies in India. The lower wages they could pay programmers in India enabled these entrepreneurs to operate their businesses at reduced costs. However, studies suggest that only perhaps 1,000 to 2,000 Indians return home from the U.S. and Canada each year—considerably fewer than the tens of thousands of Indian immigrants who arrive in America looking for a better life.

Text-Dependent Questions

1. What do Hindus consider to be the sacred scriptures?
2. What Hindu festival commemorates the triumph of good over evil?
3. How do Indian immigrants stay in touch with their families in India?

Research Project

If you are of Indian heritage, write about how your family celebrates a traditional holiday or festival, or about a specific celebration that was particularly memorable for you. If you aren't of Indian heritage, research a traditional Indian holiday or festival (such as Diwali, Navaratri Mahotsav, or India's independence day) and write a one-page report.

6 Human Smuggling and Worker Exploitation

Undocumented immigrants from India can face many serious problems in North America. If they are discovered, they face prosecution by immigration authorities; if they remain undiscovered, they are in danger of being exploited, especially by employers in search of cheap labor.

Undocumented immigrants either sneak across a border or enter a country legally but overstay their visas. They may use phony identity documents, make false *asylum* claims and then disappear while awaiting a hearing, or carry out marriage, family relation, or work visa *fraud*. It is unknown exactly how many undocumented immigrants reside in North America; analysts estimated that in 2016 there were approximately 11.3 million living in the United States.

Human Smuggling

The United States began trying to tighten its borders against illegal immigration from Asia after a rusty freighter named the *Golden Venture* ran aground in 1993 off New York's Rockaway Peninsula. Aboard the vessel were 286 Chinese immigrants, who had each paid smugglers $35,000 for passage to America. When the ship became caught on the rocks, the smugglers released the passengers into frigid ocean waters; 10 passengers died while

◀ A man apprehended after trying to illegally immigrate sits alone in a holding cell. The road from India to North America is a dangerous one for undocumented immigrants, and many of those who arrive safely still face the danger of being exploited in the workplace.

trying to swim to shore. The police and Coast Guard rescued the others.

During the 1990s the thriving economy of the United States attracted large numbers of undocumented immigrants. The majority of undocumented immigrants are Mexicans, but many also come from Asian countries, including India. According to a 2014 report by the Pew Research Center, an estimated 450,000 undocumented Indian immigrants reside in the United States. This represents about 4 percent of the total illegal immigrant population.

There have been numerous investigation to find and deport illegal immigrants. One undertaken in 1994 turned up hundreds of undocumented Indian and Pakistani immigrants in New York City. Through smugglers, the immigrants had arranged to buy fake employment and entry documents—costing between $500 and $2,000—from INS agents posing as corrupt officials. When the undocumented immigrants arrived at a warehouse to pick up their documents, the smugglers were arrested and the immigrants served with deportation notices.

In 1997, the INS dismantled a smuggling gang that was transporting about 50 undocumented immigrants, mostly from India and Pakistan, to Houston and other cities each month. The gang would receive $28,000 for each immigrant smuggled. Recruited by the smugglers in India and Pakistan, the immigrants were flown to Moscow, Russia, where it was easy to arrange flights and obtain travel papers. They then flew to Managua, Nicaragua, and from there they were driven in vans or trucks to a safe house located just south of the Texas or

 Words to Understand in This Chapter

asylum—protection granted by a nation to someone who has left their native country as a political refugee.
fraud—wrongful or criminal deception intended to result in financial or personal gain.

Arizona border. Later, guides led them across the border into the United States.

In March 1998, federal officials broke up a smuggling ring that over a seven-month period brought approximately 1,000 undocumented immigrants from India, China, and Nepal into the United States, at a charge of as much as $30,000 per individual. A yearlong federal investigation ending in November 1998 disbanded the largest immigrant smuggling cartel in U.S. history. Thirty-one people were indicted for immigration violations and money laundering. Over a three-year period, the ring brought in 300 immigrants per month, approximately 12,000 overall, mostly single men from India. The immigrant or a prospective employer paid the smugglers' fees of $20,000 to $28,000 per individual, enabling the cartel to gross about $220 million.

In the spring of 2001, the Canadian Council of Professional Engineers (CCPE) alerted immigration officials to a scam involving illegal immigration into Canada. Immigrants from India and China claiming to be engineers were entering the country using phony transcripts and resumes, then disappearing once inside the country. The CCPE had become suspicious after reviewing the false documents of a number of the immigrants.

Worker Exploitation

Actually making it to the United States or Canada does not ensure success for undocumented immigrants, as they can be taken advantage of after reaching their destination. Smugglers have been known to seize the newcomers' passports or other documents. Undocumented immigrants have been forced by threats or physical abuse to work long hours in barricaded sweatshops for pay far below minimum wage.

Often undocumented immigrants are afraid to quit their jobs because they don't know anyone in the country, don't understand the language, and have little or no money. They are reluctant to report dangerous working conditions. Uninformed about the U.S. civil rights and labor laws that protect undocumented immigrants, they seldom contact authorities for help, fearful of being deported. Smugglers or employers may set up arrangements in which workers agree to work to pay off a debt, but the employers may rig the contracts so that they never end. For instance, an employer might add on to an immigrant's debt by accusing him or her of ruining property.

Government crackdowns on smugglers protect undocumented workers and shut down shops run by corrupt employers. In the past, INS investigators worked to uphold the 1986 federal law imposing civil and criminal penalties on employers who knowingly hired undocumented immigrants. The immigrants would be detained, then deported and subsequently barred from reentering the United States for up to 10 years. These responsibilities now fall under the direction of the Bureau of Immigration and Customs Enforcement (ICE).

In February 2002, Indian immigrants filed a federal lawsuit against their former employer, the John Pickle Company of Tulsa, Oklahoma, alleging fraud, deceit, and civil rights violations. According to the suit's allegations, John Pickle, the owner of the equipment manufacturing company, hired 53 experienced Indian welders in October 2001. They had been recruited by a Mumbai employment agency called al-Samit, which required each man to borrow $2,500 at a high interest rate to pay an application fee. The new jobs promised $900 a month with overtime pay, wage raises, and good benefits. At the promised salary, the workers expected they would quickly pay off the debt and be able to support their extended families back in India.

However, upon boarding the plane the new employees were told they would have a temporary "business visit" visa instead of one that was more permanent. Also, the immigrants claimed that Pickle's wife took their passports and visas and that Pickle put them on a grueling work schedule with poor living conditions. Their complaints were answered with threats of deportation. Some of the workers attempted an escape, but were found out and nearly deported, before the INS intervened to protect them. The welders remained in Tulsa, accepting the housing assistance and food from individuals and local charities. Meanwhile, the Pickle Company denied wrongdoing, claiming it had provided clean living quarters, Indian cuisine, and an open worksite. The Equal Employment Opportunity Commission picked up the case and filed an employment discrimination lawsuit in January 2003.

In 2006, a federal court judge ruled that the Pickle Company had subjected the Indian workers to fraud and deceit, inadequate pay, sub-standard living conditions, false imprisonment, lockdowns with an armed guard, phone tapping, food rationing, restrictions on freedom to worship, degrading job assignments, ethnic slurs, intimidation, and the non-payment of wages earned. The Court ordered the Pickle Company to pay fines as well as to compensate the workers

Text-Dependent Questions

1. What was the *Golden Venture*?
2. What government agency is responsible for finding undocumented immigrants who are working in the United States?

Research Project

To become a U.S. citizen, an immigrant from another country must pass a civics test. U.S. Citizenship and Immigration Services offers practice tests at: https://my.uscis.gov/prep/test/civics/view
  Take a test. What percentage did you get correct? Do some further research about any answers you got wrong.

7 Future Immigration

In 2016 the U.S. Census Bureau reported that the country's total population was estimated at more than 325 million, with Indian Americans making up about 1 percent of the population. Canada's total population in 2016 was more than 36 million, with Asian Indians making up roughly 4 percent of the population.

Each year, about 100,000 people immigrate from India to the United States and Canada. Those immigration figures will probably remain high in the future, but much depends on what the future of India brings. Will a good Indian economy create more job opportunities, enabling more people to stay at home? Several American companies have already established operations in India, as the Internet has made *telecommuting* possible between the two countries.

On the other hand, if conditions should worsen at home, greater numbers of Indians may continue to seek new opportunities elsewhere. They may already have relatives in North America and want to follow in their footsteps. Changes in the North American economy are also factors to consider. Will conditions in the United States and Canada continue to promise a

◀ A parade celebrating India's independence day in New York City. In the coming years, it is likely that the ongoing problems and poverty in India will continue to cause Indians to emigrate to the United States and Canada.

better life? Also, how difficult will new restrictions make it for immigrants entering the country? Will they feel welcome?

Prejudice and Hate Crimes

Some people fear that changes in recent years have made the country less *hospitable* to immigrants. Much of this is due to concerns about terrorist attacks in the country, such as the 2015 mass shooting in San Bernardino, California, committed by a pair of Pakistani Americans extremists. Many Americans of Indian descent are worried that they will be being mistaken for Middle Easterners or Pakistanis and become the target of hate crimes.

Concerns about immigrants were heightened after the September 11, 2001, terrorist attacks on New York City. In the six days after the 9/11 attack, Sikhnet.com—a website that covers items of interest to the international Sikh community—reported 133 incidences of hate crime and harassment against Sikhs.

In one widely reported incident, on September 15, 2001, an Indian Sikh, Balbir Singh Sodhi, was killed outside the gas station he owned in Mesa, Arizona. The man who was eventually convicted and imprisoned for the attack told police he shot Sodhi because he wore a turban. But Sikhs weren't the only Indian Americans targeted—a Hindu temple in Matawan, New Jersey, was firebombed in the wake of the 9/11 attack, for example.

In the days and weeks after the attacks, Sikhs living in New York State distributed leaflets explaining their religion and cul-

 Words to Understand in This Chapter

hospitable—welcoming.
telecommute—to work from home, rather than an office, making use of the Internet, e-mail, and the telephone.

Indian-American Legislator

Dalip Singh Saund, a Sikh, scaled many hurdles to become the first Asian American member of Congress. The son of an illiterate contractor, he was born September 20, 1899, in Amritsar, located in northern India. Appalled to see Indian soldiers massacre civilians in 1919, he left the country and immigrated to the United States in 1920. Saund arrived with a bachelor's degree, and went on to complete two master's degrees and a doctorate at the University of California.

Settling in Imperial Valley, California, Saund found success both at ranching and in business, manufacturing, and selling chemical fertilizer. He shed his outward identity as a Sikh by shaving his beard, removing his turban, and eventually marrying a Czech American. Saund addressed local Democratic groups about India and political issues, but laws barring Asians from citizenship prevented him from running for office.

In 1942, Saund founded the Indian Association of America, which lobbied for a bill to grant citizenship to Indians. The bill passed in 1946, and in 1949 Saund became a citizen. In 1950, he was elected Westmoreland Judicial District judge, but was denied the position because he had been a citizen for less than one year. Reelected in 1951, he served as judge until 1957.

In 1956, California's Fourth District Court of Appeals rejected a petition to block Saund from running for Congress because he had been a citizen for less than seven years. He won a seat in the 29th Congressional District. In his first term, he was appointed to the House Foreign Affairs Committee. Over three terms through 1962, he worked to improve relations between the United States and India. A stroke prevented him from running for a fourth term. He died April 23, 1973, at the age of 73.

ture. Indian Prime Minister Vajpayee also asked President Bush to ensure the safety of Sikhs living in the United States. And many Americans supported the Sikh victims of hate crimes.

Immigration and the Economy

A report by the Aspen Institute's Domestic Strategy Group predicts that immigration will be an important factor in maintaining healthy U.S. economic growth. The Aspen Institute report predicts that a decrease in the U.S. population and education levels will slow the country's economic growth. In the future, industries will continue to need immigrant workers. Particular fields that will need skilled and educated workers are medicine, nursing, and high technology, a business field that employs large numbers of Indians.

A Sikh Indian American holding a tiny American flag

The National Center for Education Statistics has made similar predictions about the need for teachers in the future. Their reports estimate that by 2020 over 3 million teachers will be needed to teach students in the United States, and some education experts believe that this is yet another reason for increased immigration levels from India and other countries.

The significant impact in North America made by Indian entrepreneurs, engineers, and doctors in their respective fields is remarkable. Seeking to make better lives for themselves and their children, these immigrants have compiled a record of achievement that few could have imagined. And their futures remain bright. While the numbers of Indian immigrants are lower than those of other immigrant groups, their individual success stories show that a nation of immigrants is built one person at a time.

 Text-Dependent Questions

1. Why do some Indian Americans fear they will be the victim of hate crimes?
2. In what fields are well-educated Indian immigrants likely to be needed?

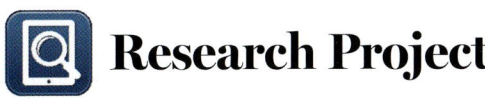 **Research Project**

Choose a famous Indian American or Indian Canadian and write a short profile of that person.

Famous Indian Americans

JAGDISH BHAGWATI (1934–), noted economist from Columbia University who has published many significant works on international trade and economics.

G. S. SHARAT CHANDRA (1938–2000), poet, translator, and fiction writer nominated for the Pulitzer Prize; literary journals such as the *Paris Review* and the *Missouri Review* published his poems, many of which dealt with the Indian immigrant experience.

DR. SUBRAHMANYAN CHANDRASEKHAR (1910–1995), astrophysicist and winner of the Nobel Prize in Physics in 1983. He discovered a phenomenon of stars that became known as the "Chandrasekhar limit"; the Chandra X-Ray telescope, used by NASA, is named after him.

KALPANA CHAWLA (1961–2003), aeronautical engineer and astronaut; became the first Indian American woman in space by serving as mission specialist aboard Space Shuttle *Columbia* Flight STS-87 in 1997. She was one of seven astronauts killed when *Columbia* exploded while re-entering Earth's atmosphere in 2003.

DEEPAK CHOPRA (1947–), best-selling author and lecturer whose theories blending Western science with ayurveda gained popularity in the 1990s; founded the Center for Well Being in La Jolla, California.

NINA DAVULURI (1989–), public speaker and activist who in September 2013 became the first Indian American to be chosen as Miss America.

HERB DHALIWAL (1952–), Canadian businessman and politician. He was the first person of South Asian descent appointed to a cabinet-level position in a Western democracy when he became minister of national revenue in 1998.

UJJAL DOSANJH (1947–), Indian Canadian lawyer and politician; became Canada's first provincial premier of Indian descent when he was elected premier of British Columbia in 2000.

DINESH D'SOUZA (1961–), best-selling author, journalist, and political scientist. From 2010 to 2012, he served as president of The King's College, a Christian school in New York City.

NIMRATA "NIKKI" RANDHAWA HALEY (1972–), politician who was elected governor of South Carolina in 2010 and re-elected in 2014. She is the second Indian American to serve as a state governor.

Piyush "Bobby" Jindal (1971–), politician who served as governor of Louisiana from 2008 to 2016. He was the first Indian American to serve as a state governor.

Vinod Khosla (1955–), cofounder of Sun Microsystems, a large technology company based in Silicon Valley, California. He also serves on the board of directors of several other companies.

Zubin Mehta (1936–), orchestra conductor born in Mumbai. He has held positions as the musical director of the Montreal Symphony, Los Angeles Philharmonic Orchestra, New York Philharmonic, and the Israel Philharmonic, for whom he became Music Director for Life in 1981.

Vivek Hallegere Murthy (1977–), American physician who has served since 2013 as the 19th Surgeon General of the United States.

Manoj Night Shyamalan (1970–), screenwriter and director, born in Pondicherry to physicians who immigrated to the United States. His most successful films include *The Sixth Sense* (1999), *Signs* (2002), *The Last Airbender* (2010), *After Earth* (2013), and *The Visit* (2015).

Menaka Thakkar (1942–), dancer, choreographer, artistic director, and teacher. Master of the Bharatanyam, Odissi, and Kuchipudi Indian classical dance forms, she founded Nrtyakala: The Canadian Academy of Indian Dance in 1974.

Tanjore Viswanathan (1927–2002), flutist and music professor, first Indian musician named a national heritage fellow by the National Endowment for the Arts. He was also founder of the Navaratri Festival, which features Indian dance and music.

Fareed Zakaria (1965–), political scientist, journalist, and editor. Former editor for *Newsweek International, Foreign Affairs Quarterly,* and *Time*. Currently hosts a program on CNN and writes a weekly column for the *Washington Post*. In January 2010, received the Padma Bhushan award from the Indian government for his contribution to the field of journalism.

Series Glossary of Key Terms

assimilate—to adopt the ways of another culture; to fully become part of a different country or society.

census—an official count of a country's population.

deport—to forcibly remove someone from a country, usually back to his or her native land.

green card—a document that denotes lawful permanent resident status in the United States.

migrant laborer—an agricultural worker who travels from region to region, taking on short-term jobs.

naturalization—the act of granting a foreign-born person citizenship.

passport—a paper or book that identifies the holder as the citizen of a country; usually required for traveling to or through other foreign lands.

undocumented immigrant—a person who enters a country without official authorization; sometimes referred to as an "illegal immigrant."

visa—official authorization that permits arrival at a port of entry but does not guarantee admission into the United States.

Further Reading

Bourke, Dale Hanson. *Immigration: Tough Questions, Direct Answers.* Downers Grove, IL: InterVarsity Press, 2014.

Chandra, G. S. Sharat. *Sari of the Gods.* Minneapolis, Minn.: Coffee House Press, 1998.

Chandra, Vikram. *Red Earth and Pouring Rain.* New York: Little, Brown & Co., 1997.

Chomsky, Aviva. *Undocumented: How Immigration Became Illegal.* Boston: Beacon Press, 2014.

Dasgupta, Shamita Das, ed. *A Patchwork Shawl: Chronicles of South Asian Women.* New Brunswick, N.J.: Rutgers University Press, 1998.

D'Souza, Dinesh. *What's So Great About America.* Washington, D.C: Regnery Publishing, 2002.

Gjelten, Tom. *A Nation of Nations: A Great American Immigration Story.* New York: Simon and Schuster, 2015.

Kamdar, Mira. *Motiba's Tattoos: A Granddaughter's Journey into Her Indian Family's Past.* New York: Plume, 2000.

Merino, Noel. *Illegal Immigration.* San Diego: Greenhaven Press, 2015.

Segal, Uma A. *A Framework for Immigration: Applications to Asians in the United States.* New York: Columbia University Press, 2002.

Internet Resources

www.uscis.gov

The website of U.S. Citizenship and Immigration Services explains the various functions of the organization and provides specific information on immigration policy.

www.canadianhistory.ca/iv/main.html

This site contains an excellent history of immigration to Canada from the 1800s to the present.

http://aianational.com

The Association of Indians in America (AIA) is the oldest national association of Asian Indians in America. The organization concerns itself with the social welfare of South Asians who have decided to live in the United States.

www.garamchai.com

A collection of links to Indian American associations, publications, temples, churches, mosques, and other websites of interest.

www.indiacurrents.com

A monthly publication covering the topics of literature, dance, music, and film that are of interest to Indian Americans.

www.indiatribune.com

The companion website of the weekly newspaper for Indian Americans that is published in Chicago, New York, and Atlanta.

Publisher's Note: The websites listed on this page were active at the time of publication. The publisher is not responsible for websites that have changed their address or discontinued operation since the date of publication. The publisher reviews and updates the websites each time the book is reprinted.

www.indiawest.com
A weekly Indian American newsmagazine featuring coverage of events and developments in India.

www.littleindia.com
A monthly feature magazine with articles on Indian life outside of India.

www.indius.org
Indian Americans Involved in the U.S (IndiUS) is a forum created to share news and articles that promote the culture of Indian Americans and encourage community involvement.

www.newsindia-times.com
A New York–based newspaper reporting on issues of interest to the Indian community.

www.rediff.com
A media and Internet company with comprehensive resources for the Indian American community.

www.iado.org
The homesite of the Indo-American Democratic Organization (IADO), a lobby group that serves Indian Americans and is engaged in issues concerning them, including immigration, education, and hate crimes.

www.cia.gov/library/publications/the-world-factbook/geos/in.html
The CIA World Factbook's India page.

Index

1976 Immigration Act (Canada), 50
1952 Immigration and Nationality Act, 43
1965 Immigration and Nationality Act, **42**, 44, 52
1986 Immigration Reform and Control Act, 44

American Association of Physicians of Indian Origin, 61, 68
Asian American Hotel Owners Association, 68
Asian Indian Historical Archive Committee, 78–79
Association of Indians in America (AIA), 67
Atlanta, Ga., 62, **63**, 68
Ayodhya, India, 28
ayurveda, 20–21
    See also Hinduism

Balakrishnan, Ajit, 67
Bangalore, India, 36–37
Baqi, Mir, 28
Bhagwati, Jagdish, 98
Bharat. See India
Bharatiya Janata Party, 27, **28**
    See also Hinduism
Blaise, Clark, 79
Bollywood, 83–84
    See also culture
Bombay. See Mumbai, India
Buddhism, 75–76, 77
    See also religion
Bureau of Citizenship and Immigration Services (BCIS), 46
Bureau of Customs and Border Protection (BCBP), 46
Bureau of Immigration and Customs Enforcement (BICE), 46, 90
Bush, George W., **45**, 94–95
Business 2.0, 54

Calcutta, India, 25

Canada
    immigration history, 48–51
    immigration rates, 17, 55
    Indian communities, 65–66
    Indian population in, 15, 17, 18, 49, 66, 93, **95**
Caste and Outcast (Mukerji), 19
caste system, **23**, 26–27, 28, 72, 73, 75
    See also Hinduism
Chandra, G. S. Sharat, 79, 98
Chandrasekhar, Subrahmanyan, 98
Chawla, Kalpana, 98
Chicago, Ill., 55, 60–62, 81
Chinese Exclusion Act of 1882, 39–40, **41**
Chopra, Deepak, 98
Christianity, 30
    See also religion
Citizenship and Immigration Canada (CIC), 18
Cleveland, Ohio, **52**, 55, 63
communities, 59–66
Coward, Harold, 49
cuisine, Indian, 18–19, 77–78
    See also culture
culture, 18–21, 76–85
    See also religion

Days and Nights in Calcutta (Blaise and Mukherjee), 79
Department of Homeland Security, 45–46, 54
Dhaliwal, Herb, 49, 98
discrimination, 94–96
Displaced Persons Act of 1948, 43
    See also refugees
Diwali, **79**, 80–81
    See also holidays
Dosanjh, Ujjal, 98
D'Souza, Dinesh, 98

East India Company, 23
    See also Great Britain

Numbers in ***bold italic*** refer to captions.

economy
    Indian, 34–37
    United States, 96–97
Education Week, 54
employment, 17, 18, 52–54, **57**, 58, 59, 66–67, 85, 90–91, 97
Enhanced Border Security and Visa Entry Reform Act (2002), 45
ethnicity, 23, 39–41, 48
    See also quotas

Fermi, Laura, 42–43
Festival of Lights. *See* Diwali
"Festival of Nine Nights" (Navaratri Mahotsav), 82
        See also holidays

Gandhi, Indira, 31
Gandhi, Mohandas, 23–24, 27, 28
Gandhi, Sonia, **74**
Gautama, Siddhartha, 76
Gay Neck: The Story of a Pigeon (Mukerji), 19
Ghond the Hunter (Mukerji), 19
Gilmore, Rachna, 78, 81
Global Organization of People of Indian Origin, 68
Golden Venture, 87–88
    See also undocumented immigrants
Grant, Madison, 42
Great Britain, 23–24, 32, 49, 81
Gujarat, India, 59, 60, 62, 63
Gujarati Samaj of Tampa Bay Association, 62

H-1B visas, 54
    See also visas
Hare Krishna movement, **75**
    See also religion
Harrison, George, **75**
Hindu Temple Society of North America, 72
        See also Hinduism
Hinduism, 16, 19, 20, 23, 26, 27–31, 32–33, 71–72, 75, 76, 77, 82
    and Diwali, 80–81
        See also religion
holidays, **79**, 80–81
    See also culture
Homeland Security Act of 2002, 45
Houston, Tex., 64–65
human smuggling, 88–90
    See also undocumented immigrants

Illegal Immigration Reform and Immigrant Responsibility Act (1996), 45
immigration
    difficulties of, 84–85
    history of, in Canada, 48–51
    history of, in the United States, 39–48, 51–52
    rates of, in Canada, 17, 55
    rates of, in the United States, 16–17, 39, **40**, 43, 46–47, 51, 53, 54–55, **96**
    reasons for, 16, 59, 93
Immigration Act of 1924, 42
    See also quotas
Immigration Act of 1990, 44
Immigration Act of 1952 (Canada), 50
Immigration and Nationality Act of 1952, 43
Immigration and Nationality Act of 1965, **42**, 44, 52
Immigration and Naturalization Service (INS), 44, 88, 90
    See also Department of Homeland Security
Immigration and Refugee Protection Act (Canada), 50–51
Immigration Reform and Control Act (1986), 44
Independence Day (August 15), 81
    See also holidays
India, 15–16
    economy, 34–37
    history, 23–24, 28–31, 32–34
    and Pakistan, 32–34
    population, 24–26
India Association of Cleveland, 63
India Association of St. Louis, 64
India Canada Association, 67
India Community Center, 64
India Cultural Center (Tampa, Fla.), 61, 63
Indian Americans
    communities, 59–66
    discrimination against, 94–96
    education, 17, 18, 53, 59
    employment, 17, 18, 52–54, **57**, 58, 59, 66–67, 85, 90–91, 97
    population, 15, 16–17, 53, **58**, 59, 61, 93
        See also culture
Indian Association of America, 94
Indo-America Charity Foundation, 65
Indo-American Association, 65
Indo-American Center, 62

Indo-American Chamber of Commerce of Greater Houston, 65
IndUS Entrepreneurs, 68–69
The Industry Standard, 85
Islam, 23, 26, 27–30, 32–33, 71, 73
   See also religion

Jainism, 71, 73, 77
   See also religion
Jamaat-i-Islami, **33**
Jammu, 32, 34
John Pickle Company, 90–91
   See also employment
Johnson, Lyndon B., **42**, 52
Joshi, Akashata, **37**

Kari the Elephant (Mukerji), 19
Kashmir, 32–34, **93**
Khalistan, 30
Khalsa Diwan Society, 66
Khosla, Vinod, 53–54, 98
Komagata Maru, 49
Kraus, Clifford, 65–66

Lahiri, Jhumpa, 84–85
language, 24, 26
Laughlin, Harry D., 41
Lights for Gita (Gilmore), 78, 81
Little Indias, 60, 66
   See also communities
The Lotus, 64

Mahatma Gandhi Center, 64
Mahavira, 73
   See also Jainism
mehndi, 20
   See also culture
Mehta, Zubin, 99
Montreal, Quebec, 65, 66
Mother India, **83**, 84
Mukerji, Dhan Gopal, 19
Mukherjee, Bharati, 79
Mumbai, India, 24–25, 35, 59, 74, 78

Nanak, 75
   See also Sikhism
National Indo-American Hospitality Association, 68
Natya Shastras, 82
   See also culture
Navaratri Mahotsav ("Festival of Nine Nights"), 82

   See also holidays
Nehru, Pandit Jawaharlal, **24**
New Delhi, India, 24, 31, 34, 35
New York City, N.Y., 59–60, 81
New York Times, 66, 67
Newsweek International, 84

Open Doors, 18
organizations, 60, 62–65, 66, 67–69, 81–82

Pakistan, 32–34, **93**
Palo Alto, Calif., 17
Parsism, 71, 73–74
   See also religion
Patel, Kiran C., 61
Patel, Pallavi, 61
Pearson, Lester, 50
points system, 50–51
   See also Canada
population
   India, 24–26
   Indian American, 15, 16–17, 53, **58**, 59, 61, 93
   Indian Canadian, 15, 17, 18, 49, 66, 93, **95**
Powell, Colin, 32
Prabhupada, A. C. Bhaktivedanta Swami, 75

quotas, 39, 40–41, 42–44
   See also immigration

Refugee Act of 1980, 44
refugees, 43, 44, 48, 50–51, 55
religion, 16, 19, 20, 23, 26, 27–31, 32–33, 71–76, 77, 80–82
Republic of India. *See* India

Sabarmati Express, 29–30
San Francisco, Calif., 81
San Francisco Bay Area Federation of Indo-American Associations, 60
San Jose, Calif., 17
Sangh Parivar (United Family), 30
   See also Hinduism
Sarhali, Gurdt Singh, 49
Sari of the Gods (Chandra), 79
Saund, Dalip Singh, 94
Saxenian, AnnaLee, 53
Scully, C. D., 41
Sharma, Shruti, **80**
Shyamalan, Manoj Night, 99
Sikhism, 71, 75

See also religion
Sikhs, 30–31, 49, 55, **57**, **65**, 66, **71**, **74**, 94–96
Singh, Beant, 31
Singh, Gobind, 75
   See also Sikhism
Sodhi, Balbir Singh, 95–96
Soni, Gorthandas, 77
St. Louis, Mo., 64

Tampa, Fla., 61, 62–63
Temporary Quota Act of 1921, 42
   See also quotas
Thakkar, Menaka, 99
Time Select/Global Business Report, 17–18
Toronto, Ontario, 65–66

undocumented immigrants, 44, 46, 47, 87–91
United Family (Sangh Parivar), 30
   See also Hinduism
United States
   economy, 96–97
   immigration rates, 16–17, 39, **40**, 43, 46–47, 51, 53, 54–55, **96**
   Indian population in, 15, 16–17, 53, **58**, 59, 61, 93
USA PATRIOT Act (2002), 45

Vajpayee, Atal Bihari, 27, **28**, 94–95
Vancouver, British Columbia, 49, **65**, 66, **71**
Vedanta Society, 16
   See also Hinduism
Victoria, British Columbia, 49
visas, 41, 44, 47, 54
   See also immigration
Viswanathan, Tanjore, 99
Vivekananda, Hindu Swami, 16
   See also Hinduism

The Wasp, **41**
World War II, 41, 48

yoga, 16, 21
   See also ayurveda
Yogi, Maharishi Mahesh, 20, **21**
   See also ayurveda

Zakaria, Fareed, 98

Contributors

Senior consulting editor **STUART ANDERSON** is an adjunct scholar at the Cato Institute and executive director of the National Foundation for American Policy. From August 2001 to January 2003, he served as executive associate commissioner for Policy and Planning and Counselor to the Commissioner at the Immigration and Naturalization Service. He spent four and a half years on Capitol Hill on the Senate Immigration Subcommittee, first for Senator Spencer Abraham and then as Staff Director of the subcommittee for Senator Sam Brownback. Prior to that, Stuart was Director of Trade and Immigration Studies at the Cato Institute, where he produced reports on the military contributions of immigrants and the role of immigrants in high technology. Stuart has published articles in the Wall Street Journal, New York Times, Los Angeles Times, and other publications. He has an M.A. from Georgetown University and a B.A. in Political Science from Drew University. His articles have appeared in such publications as the *Wall Street Journal*, *New York Times*, and *Los Angeles Times*.

MARIAN L. SMITH served as the senior historian of the U.S. Immigration and Naturalization Service (INS) from 1988 to 2003, and is currently the immigration and naturalization historian within the Department of Homeland Security in Washington, D.C. She studies, publishes, and speaks on the history of the immigration agency and is active in the management of official 20th-century immigration records.

PETER HAMMERSCHMIDT is director general of national cyber security at Public Safety Canada. He previously served as First Secretary (Financial and Military Affairs) for the Permanent Mission of Canada to the United Nations. Before taking this position, he was a ministerial speechwriter and policy specialist for the Department of National Defence in Ottawa. Prior to joining the public service, he served as the Publications Director for the Canadian Institute of Strategic Studies in Toronto. He has a B.A. (Honours) in Political Studies from Queen's University, and an MScEcon in Strategic Studies from the University of Wales, Aberystwyth.

TOM BALOG is a freelance writer and editor. He is a resident of Chicago, where he lives with his wife Alison. This is his first book.

Picture Credits

Page
- 1: used under license from Shutterstock, Inc.
- 2: used under license from Shutterstock, Inc.
- 9: used under license from Shutterstock, Inc.
- 12: Stacey Newman / Shutterstock.com
- 14: Ami Vitale/Getty Images
- 17: used under license from Shutterstock, Inc.
- 18: used under license from Shutterstock, Inc.
- 19: used under license from Shutterstock, Inc.
- 20: Corbis Images
- 22: Sean Pavone / Shutterstock.com
- 24: AsiaTravel / Shutterstock.com
- 27: Travel Stock / Shutterstock.com
- 28: Hulton/Archive/Getty Images
- 31: Maodoltee / Shutterstock.com
- 33: Natalia Davidovich / Shutterstock.com
- 34: Asianet-Pakistan / Shutterstock.com
- 36: Daniel J. Rao / Shutterstock.com
- 37: Hung Chung Chih / Shutterstock.com
- 38: Paul Prescott / Shutterstock.com
- 40: Hulton/Archive/Getty Images
- 43: Library of Congress
- 44: used under license from Shutterstock, Inc.
- 46: courtesy Lyndon B. Johnson Library
- 48: Alex Wong/Getty Images
- 58: Nick Starichenko / Shutterstock.com
- 61: A. Katz / Shutterstock.com
- 62: Gail Mooney/Corbis
- 64: used under license from Shutterstock, Inc.
- 67: Mikecphoto / Shutterstock.com
- 69: Rich Koele / Shutterstock.com
- 72: Dave G. Houser/Corbis
- 75: Nisargmedia.com / Shutterstock.com
- 76: Kaesler Media / Shutterstock.com
- 77: used under license from Shutterstock, Inc.
- 78: IMS Communications, Ltd.
- 83: Ritu Manoj Jethani / Shutterstock.com
- 84: Ilona Ignatova / Shutterstock.com
- 88: David Turnley/Corbis
- 94: Ritu Manoj Jethani / Shutterstock.com
- 98: Joseph Sohm / Shutterstock.com
- 106: used under license from Shutterstock, Inc.